Listening for Water

Sandra Wallman

Matador
9 Priory Business Park,
Wistow Road, Kibworth Beauchamp,
Leicestershire. LE8 0RX
Tel: 0116 279 2299
Email: books@troubador.co.uk
Web: www.troubador.co.uk/matador
Twitter: @matadorbooks

ISBN 978 1785893 827

British Library Cataloguing in Publication Data.
A catalogue record for this book is available from the British Library.

Printed and bound by CPI Group (UK) Ltd, Croydon, CR0 4YY
Typeset in 11pt Aldine401 by Troubador Publishing Ltd, Leicester, UK

Matador is an imprint of Troubador Publishing Ltd

…for kith and kin…

Contents

Hitchhiker

Soon as I asked, they let me out at the next slip road. Probably stupid to get into a car with three hefty G.I.s in the first place. Soon clear too that they were drinking, showing off the Chevy's mini-bar, celebrating forty-eight hours' R&R away from the American base. Friendly as puppy dogs. A bit slobbery too – and close up, even bigger than before. I felt a punch of anxiety when the freckled one made a tentative lurch. But then the dark one on the other side of me shoved at him with "Hey man. This here's a *nice* girl", and they all subsided, nodding into their bourbon and ginger ale, remembering their girls back home.

Proper danger came when the blond one driving got tearful and his steering began to wobble. That's when I asked to get out. Anyway, I never meant to go the whole way to Berlin on the autobahn. I wanted to see the real Germany. In fact I had left the others in Frankfurt only because they didn't. Quite rude about my Berlin-and-the-countryside-around-it proposal. We'll meet up later…

It is good to be alone. The motorway has faded and I hear only summer silence and birdsong. A sign points eight kilometres to the next village; there's bound to be a small *gasthof* and gentle rural people sipping something cool at the end of a morning's work in their fields. But now, nearly noon, it is getting hot. How long is a kilometre anyway?

As I remember it, round about then the chug-chug of the milk van approached. As it got closer a second layer of sound came into earshot; now there was a heavy hum and a steady rattling under the chugging. The bottles settled and the rattling stopped as the van pulled up beside me. Its idling was quieter but still loud enough to smother the voice of the old man sitting high and alone in the open cabin. Lip and gesture reading wasn't hard.

"*Grüß Gott,*" he mouthed. I mouthed it back. He flashed a whiskery smile. Then a much longer communication – no doubt involving more German than I would have understood if it were audible – with arm–waving and pointing up the road: Would I like a lift to the village? I nodded, yes and thanks, and heaved my rucksack on to the steep step of the driver's cabin.

The old man leaned across to pull the bag in, then extended his hand to help me up. Dry and rough-skinned but strong; he looked too old to have that kind of strength. Closer up his face was weathered with deep lines, dark-etched by the dust of the road. Friendly.

We nod and smile at each other across the heavy gearbox. My host now faces the road, his neck extended, tortoise-like, and we lumber off. Chitchat is not possible. I relax into the rhythm of the van, leaning out my side to catch some breeze. There is no windowpane in the door;

too much noise to hear birds, but I can smell the fields. Is it wheat? So calm and tidy. Proper countryside, this. Better than those joyriding Yanks on the stinking autobahn.

I must've dozed off. There's a scuffling kind of movement next to me, more a draught of air than a sound. The old man, still craning forward, now has only one hand on the wheel. With the other, he is lowering his trousers. Already the right leg is almost free. Shit. He's aware of me looking, and turns to look back, still struggling with the trousers. The once-sweet old-man face is now sweaty red. He is nodding at me, with his eyebrows raised and his eyes wide in a question. Good God – he's flirting! This is not scary; this is sick. The leg angling toward me is draped in loose folds of greyish flannel. Looks like that Shar-Pei dog in the advert. But this is long johns. And filthy. And it's summer…

I shake my head against his nodding question. I signal that I want to get out. *Really?* say his eyebrows. He shrugs sadly, draws the grotesque leg back to his side and manoeuvres the van to a deafening halt. I wrestle the door open and shove my rucksack over the side.

"Thank you," I say, before following it. "*Danke schön.*"

He can't hear me but reads my mouthing, says, "*Bitte sehr*" in reply. We are cordial, formal, ludicrous… The van rattles and chugs away, fading towards the village.

Not a good day, this. I'll sit here in the shade for a while. There's bound to be a sane and safe and beautiful lift around the corner.

The Golden Gate

Strolling over the lovely bridge to walk off Sunday lunch. Early autumn but no mist. Wind of course, but not a mean one – rather the sort that makes you wish for a kite. Six of us straggling in ones and twos, talking rubbish and life. Or not talking. Smiling at each other, at the perfect day. Half a mile in I dawdle to lean on the railing. The dark blue of the Bay and the ruddy red of the girders set each other off in the sun. Even the giddy drop from bridge to water, red to blue, has no menace in it: there's a ledge outside the barrier that stops you looking straight down. Not wide, only a foot or so – made for a repainting person to stand on; for me to feel safe when I look over the edge.

So for a minute I'm not alarmed to see a woman walking purposefully along it towards me. No reason why she shouldn't be there, out walking like the rest of us; neat in Sunday-clean jeans and zip-up windbreaker, pale yellow, with a small rucksack over her inside shoulder. Only when she has passed – I have stepped back from the barrier to cancel the small overhang of my hands across her path – only then the wrongness of it rises in front of me like a clearing Polaroid: she is not old but her face is grey; she holds her eyes wide and fixed forward, paying no attention to her footing on the narrow ledge; there's not been a flicker of response to me or my "Hi!". And – sweet Jesus! – there is nothing between her and hard water 220 feet below.

I run to catch up with the others. They and I and the woman, reach the centre of the bridge at the same time. The woman sits down carefully on the ledge, the rucksack neat beside her, her feet hanging over nothing. Now she stares outward to the horizon, enclosed, apparently unaware of people silting up on the bridge behind her.

For two beats the weird calm of her holds us in thrall. Then someone passing asks "You guys OK?" and the spell is broken. The six of us begin to dart about, useless in panic – "Do something! Do something!" – until someone – whose voice was it? – changes the key. "It's OK! It'll be alright! It's OK! It's alright."

It isn't of course, but the liturgy response pulls us back into pattern – a dance-like sequence in which the men hold their places and the women peel away at speed. There is no plan; on automatic, each of us does what they do. The three men stand close, backs to the water, protecting the ledge-person from the gawping crowd. We women divide: Cinda, trained in Samaritan calls, passes behind the men and squats by the railing to talk to the woman on the ledge. Marion, always practical and quick, runs to the right along the bridge to find someone who will fix this. And I run to the left, keen to be helpful but with no idea what to do. An onlooker says this kind of thing happens all the time: twenty-four damn jumpers last year.

The city does seem to be ready for this kind of thing. Every so many yards along the bridge railing there's a telephone bright with the words *Emergency Services* in big letters, and smaller, *direct, free connection*. My operator is unexcited. She thanks me for the call and asks which number telephone I'm at. She says a specialist will be with us right away. She says be careful not to scare the lady. She says we shouldn't worry. Marion, on the next telephone along, has had the same exchange with a similar person. We have done our job, is the message. Now let the experts do theirs.

Cinda squats on the ground, level with the ledge-woman, talking to her through a gap between struts in the red iron railing. She has her hands gripped on the struts and her face pressed up against them. In this position her mouth is a handspan from the woman's ear but she makes no move to touch her. I can't hear what Cinda says, but I see that the woman is inclined toward her, attentive. She nods and says something, listens a moment, then speaks again. And help is finally here. Surely now everything will be alright...

The emergency sirens come closer, one from each end of the bridge. Two vans pull off the road, blocking the sidewalk left and right, their roof lights flashing. Six or seven uniformed policemen set about controlling the eager onlookers, moving them along. One stands a bit apart, quite still looking towards Cinda and the woman. Very deliberately he takes off his cap and tucks it into

6

his belt. He is leather-clad like the others, but without the cap I see he is younger, round-faced, pink-cheeked; nervous as the others are not. One of the older officers pats him lightly on the shoulder, nudging him forward, and watches him cross the six or eight feet of sidewalk between his van and the railing.

Cinda doesn't yet notice the chaos behind her; her back stays rigid with concentration. But the woman on the ledge has become aware of it and is no longer held by Cinda's focus. Alert as a rabbit, she moves minutely away. The young officer, firm but polite, asks Cinda please to step aside. She gets up stiffly, still turned toward the woman on the ledge but relieved, she said later, to pass the baton to the proper emergency services. Here at last is the specialist, an arm's length from her and from the woman behind the railing, poised to take charge.

"Her name is Emily," Cinda tells him. She steps away and he moves into her place. The sun on the water is suddenly dazzling.

It happens in a blur. The young officer, loud enough for the clutch of us to hear, says something like "Hi, Emily. My name is Ken. C'mon now; give me your hand and we can sort this out."

I am deafened by the noise of my heart, half-blinded by what I can see. He is standing above her, his arm extended over the rail. She draws back from it and stands up, swaying a little, one hand still holding the bridge, the other at her throat. A sudden heavy gust lifts her hair. He grabs at her, achieving a yellow fistful of windbreaker. In the same second she unzips it, shrugs out of it and steps off the ledge.

At first there is only silence. Slowly sounds build up, layering on each other as they do to start a movie: Cinda retching, gasping for air; young Ken, kneeling on the ground now, whimpering over the jacket in his hands; the older officer, again with a hand on his shoulder, murmuring awkward comfort; a man's voice on a phone in one of the vans, calling up a rescue boat; the fading buzz of conversation as walkers move on, shaking their heads, hurrying their children.

We six hung about awhile. One of the police vans left, sirens ablaze as before. But it wasn't finished for us. It felt as though there was still something to be done, that it wasn't over, that Emily – now she had a name – that Emily could still be saved. The same avuncular officer was sympathetic. Yes, it is true that some people survive the fall. Not many. Maybe two per cent. We shouldn't expect it. He said they had found 'details' in Emily's rucksack and would contact the family, but that he could tell us nothing more. When Cinda said she'd like the family to know about that last conversation, that it might help them, he gave us a number to call after eight o'clock. By then, he said, the Registry will have processed Emily's case. In the event they reported that she had died on impact, and that her next of kin wanted no contact with any of us.

As the nice officer turned to join his colleagues in the waiting van, Marion asked about Ken. "He must be distraught," she said. "So terrible to lose someone like that."

"Yes," said the officer. "But it's the job. He'll get used to it. Today was extra hard. It was his first time in the front line."

Molefi's Moment

Two weeks from Saturday the Pope's visit will kick off with a rally in Maseru football ground. This is better than Christmas! Since he was an altar boy Molefi has dreamt of meeting His Holiness. Still sometimes, triggered by the smiling Technicolor likeness in its gold frame next to the chimney, in the spot his grandfather chose, he feels that same longing. Now he smiles back at the picture and takes proper time to cross himself in front of it.

In that moment, as though the Pope spoke out loud to him, Molefi remembers his grandfather's words. They were sayings the old man used to make the young ones know there could be a future better than the stingy present and, in a sideways way, to encourage effort and godliness and good behaviour at school.

"One day" – he said it often – "one day the fat lady will start singing and your ship will come in."

Two weeks from Saturday will be that special day – the Pope is one thing; even to see the real Holiness person from a distance must be a thrilling thing – but more, the Pope brings the business opportunity Molefi's been waiting for. Hundreds of people will flock to greet the Holy Father. And in the hours of speeches and prayers and blessings, some of them, maybe all of them, will grow hungry. This is the moment his grandfather promised. Molefi will be ready for it; he will have food ready to sell; he will pray hard to make it happen.

Lindiwe glows extra when he tells her the plan. In her mind she sees enough money for years of school fees. And maybe for curtains. Molefi's a good husband; she will help him to prepare the things, and to cook and to sell. It must be proper food – good meat, hot and fried on the spot so that the smell will tantalise the noses of the faithful; big hamburgers in soft buns, with a jumbo jar of mustard on the side and some crates of cool Fanta ready to buy when you want to wash it all down. Her brother Tsepo will look after drinks – he knows how to get them on sale or return.

How many hamburgers should they cook? Half the population is Protestant so *they* won't come; many Catholics live too far from Maseru, and some nearby will go to the Pope's Mass on Sunday and not bother with the welcome event... Even so, there is talk of two thousand people at the stadium. If luck is bad and only half of them buy, one burger each, that's still a thousand. A thousand is without risk. Some may even eat more than one. If the supply runs out people will be disappointed but they must be turned away. Lindiwe knows you can make seven good hamburgers from one pound of meat. Seven into one thousand... Molefi will need 150 pounds of minced beef. And a thousand buns.

He visits his cousin Moeketsi who works in the abattoir. They drink and talk together. Moeketsi's eyes go wide when he hears the plan, but he says, OK, he will speak to *Baas* Hendrik, the one in charge, on Molefi's behalf; to open the talk. So he relays the message: that there could be an order for 150 pounds of good beef, minced ready for hamburgers…

The boss wants to see Molefi in person.

He's glad he went for the meeting in his suit. *Baas* Hendrik says yes, he will do it. The price – he says it's a special price for the Pope's visit – will be four rands each pound, including mincing and delivery to the stadium. And of course the money, the R600, must be paid upfront, in cash, no questions. Molefi has never seen money like that; the best wage he has ever earned is R20 for a month. But this is a different story; this is business, and with business comes a different life.

Then the buns. Mme Sophia in the small shop says her ovens could make three hundred, some the day before, but not a thousand. Ten cents each for bulk, so R30 please. The foreman at United Bakeries, a friend of Molefi's father's brother, can match her price for the rest if he runs the ovens outside normal hours, as a favour.

So the meat will cost R600 and the buns will cost R100. Add R80 for two gas bottles, plus ten pounds of lard, three jumbo mustards and miscellaneous extras – onions, maybe – of course onions – and paper napkins – altogether another hundred. So R880. Say R900 to be safe.

The only body with so much money to lend is the

bank. Molefi has no connecting person to help him in, but no matter. This very bank has been advertising loans for *small business development, offered at helpful rates of interest to clients with appropriate collateral*. That's in case the business can't pay back. Of course it will, but he can put his house on the table to cover it. It's a small house, but a strong one, with a corrugated tin roof and a water tap in the yard; his brother and two friends helped him build it when he was ready to marry. Also, there's the bicycle – but the house will be enough. A house this good can be worth maybe even two thousand rands! And he only needs nine hundred! And only for one month!

Molefi puts all the costings down on a paper. He shows how he has divided the R880 by a thousand hamburgers so that each hamburger costs less than one rand. He puts the selling price at three – cheaper than McDonalds in South Africa, and the food will be better, on-the-spot fresh. He practises how he will tell these numbers to the bank. Next day he goes there to make the appointment, and on the way home he passes by Tsepo's to borrow his good white shirt. At home, Lindiwe has sponged the suit and pressed it with a flat iron heated on the gas ring.

The day after, looking sharp, feeling fit, Molefi knocks at the bank manager's door exactly on time.

The manager is a Catholic and even courteous; he has verified that Molefi goes to Mass every week, that he is a solid married man with a child and has no debts. The manager tends to agree that a large crowd of believers will turn up at the stadium. Moreover – this he doesn't say aloud – Head Office is starting to ask why he has as yet produced no candidates for the business development offer. Molefi, you could say, is a godsend. The manager is not quite convinced of the size of the hamburger market – perhaps because he doesn't himself like hamburgers – but Molefi's collateral is ample and the bank risks nothing by advancing the sum he asks for.

The secretary types it up: principal sum, period of loan, rate of interest. The two men sign their papers and the secretary brings the money. Molefi puts it in his inner pocket and signs again for the receipt. All done, he shakes the manager's hand and floats from the bank.

Now it is the Pope's Saturday. Late last night Molefi made two trips on his bicycle to collect the buns, and this morning he is awake before sun-up to carry his sleeping child to the neighbour's. Tsepo and Moeketsi arrive almost at once, and Lindiwe is ready with bread and tea. The four of them joke and tease one another while they load and push Molefi's bicycle and Tsepo's handcart between the house and the stadium. They make several trips – one to bring the Fanta drinks from Tsepo's yard – and by seven o'clock the table is assembled, the gas burner connected and the shiny cooking pans in position. On the ground in front of the table there's a signboard which Moeketsi has painted; he is the one who did good drawing in school.

POPE'S SPECIAL
BEST HAMBURGERS FRESH COOKED
HELP YOURSELF TO MUSTARD
BUNS AND ONIONS INCLUDED
TODAY ONLY R3

The stall is inside the stadium near the main entrance – not far from the toilet block, but not too close. It is six feet long, made of three wide and sturdy planks which rest on a pair of trestles borrowed from the school hall. The table is shaded full-length by two faded beach umbrellas which the petrol garage that was once also a cafe no longer uses. Lindiwe has revived them with yards of bright paper chain. She was happy cutting and pasting with the child. It was like a game, and they laughed together. She waited till he slept to chop the onions – five big basins full; her eyes are sore from onion juice and heavy with lack of sleep, but this morning the sound of those paper chains rustling in the rising breeze is cheerful. Festive, even…

Eight o'clock, as promised, a flatbed truck pulls up outside the entrance. *Baas* Hendrik himself gets out, openly curious, taking in the sign and the gas burner and the bunting and Lindiwe's white apron. He nods, maybe approving, but probably he doesn't care how things look or how they'll turn out because Molefi paid him his full money more than a week ago. He signals the elderly boy driving with him to open the back and six bloody packages are wrestled to the ground and stacked under the table. They are cold still, and the meat is minced fine. Moeketsi climbs into their place on the open truck to take a lift into work. He makes a boxer's victory sign over his head as the truck pulls away.

The Pope's event doesn't start till two o'clock, but people will come sooner to get a place where they can see him, so a batch of food must be ready before. Lindiwe uses a pound packet of lard to estimate a pound of raw mince, balancing one against the other in her hands. She divides each pound into seven blobs, lining them up on a clean paper. The men then mix each blob with a spoon of onion and pat it into a hamburger shape. They work through fourteen pounds of meat in this way. After a couple of hours a hundred hamburgers are lined up for cooking, a hundred buns are slit to receive them, and everything is covered with clean cloths against the dust and the flies. Now just to wait.

They pass an easy half hour sitting on the wooden bottle crates drinking Fanta and squinting at the weather. The meat will suffer as the day gets hotter; it is the time of year for heat.

Lindiwe observes that the rains will soon follow and she must plant pumpkins. "Rain is a blessing; perhaps the Pope will call it down for us."

Anyway, when he arrives everyone will shout the national greeting: *Khotso! Pula! Nala!* – Peace, Rain, Prosperity – and such force of welcome in his presence could make rain come.

Molefi says rain's not always good; it can be too much. Think how thunder and lightning come fierce across the mountains to destroy the mealies and kill cattle. Tsepo tells again how he was caught in that storm last year and had to lie flat on the ground for an hour to be safe from it. The others nod, remembering. Molefi says there'll be no storm like that today; not even rain.

Just after 11.30 a small van arrives; two men carrying audio equipment for the stage greet them as they pass the stall. Half a dozen children scatter in behind them. The one who can read says three rand is a pity; he likes meat too much... It's time for action. Molefi lights the burner, spoons in a dollop of lard and sets the first six hamburgers to cook.

From noon the faithful begin to come – a steady trickle, but sparse. Just after two o'clock, when the Pope's open car drives through the entrance gates and up to the platform steps, there is an audience of no more than four hundred waiting for him. Some cross themselves as he passes – mostly older people, mostly women; everyone joins in to raise the greeting as he stands to bless the crowd – *Khotso! Pula! Nala!* The sound rises bravely up and over the stadium walls.

Lindiwe crosses herself as the Pope drives by the hamburger stall on the way in, and the three of them mumble the greeting when he stands, but their enthusiasm is pale. Up to this moment they have sold forty-two hamburgers; the morning's first batch is less than half gone. Those who bought a hamburger have been happy; two men even came back for a second one. But there are not enough people here, and not enough of them want to buy. Already the heat is too much, and the meat is suffering Perhaps on the way out people will stop for food?

The most senior of the Catholic chiefs makes a

speech to introduce the day, and then invites each one of three church dignitaries, in order of rank, to address the Pope and the Nation. They are by custom eloquent speakers, and their listeners know to stand still and be quiet. When finally it's the Pope's turn the audience pays full attention, inclining towards the stage, some again crossing themselves, responding with one voice to the litany. Many words are spoken and it is close to four o'clock before the orations and the prayers and the Pope's blessings run out. Once more everyone cheers him – *Khotso! Pula! Nala!*

As he comes down from the platform there is a collective sigh and a swirl of movement as the crowd turns, ready to follow him out of the stadium. This time he goes on foot, looking left and right and waving his hand in a half-circle from the wrist. The car drives slowly in front of him; he is flanked by the senior chief and the priests and two large laymen who will prevent any crush, and by four altar boys who hold an awning over his head to protect the holy whiteness of him from the sun.

Lindiwe and Tsepo stand behind the table ready to sell. Molefi moves forward and cranes to see the procession coming. At first his view is blocked by the car, then suddenly the Pope is there, level with the stall. He has slowed down and is reading the hamburger sign. He signals that he will approach it and the small entourage adjusts to let him through. Once close enough he stands quite still, giving each part of the scene his full attention – the cheerful bunting, the ready burgers, the stack of buns, the bleeding packages under the table…

For a long minute Molefi doesn't breathe. Now the Pope is in front of him and proffering his hand. Molefi somehow knows he should genuflect and kiss the Pope's ring; that he should look at the ground.

The Pope says, just to him, "I bless your brave spirit, my son", and quietly, not for the crowd, he intones the special words *"In Nomine Patris…"* as he makes the sign of the cross over Molefi's bowed head. Then he moves back into the stream of people and leads them out of the football ground.

Walking By

New Year's Day in Amsterdam. We are heading west on Rozenstraat, trying not to look into ground floor windows which open straight on to the cobbled road. Some of them are barred, but still, private and public spaces merge. Also, there is no clear line between the people's path and the part for cars. The unpretty outcome of this is a solid rank of vehicles parked along the left hand side of the road.

We are strolling, loosely four abreast, sub-setting into ones and twos when the way narrows or the talk fragments. Gradually, not like a sudden interruption, there is another voice in the mix. A woman.

"Hey," she is saying. And again, "Hey."

We stop to place the sound.

"Hey," she says. "Yes. You people passing. It's me you hear. I want help. Please will somebody help me?"

The voice is some ten metres behind us. Three of us are rooted where we stand, looking vaguely about – not afraid, just slow to react. But Pieter, always quick, live always to every detail and every person's need, immediately turns back, finds the right gap between the parked cars and threads his way through to face the voice. By the time he has unravelled the proper sequence of formal greeting, the rest of us begin to straggle nearer. Each of us keeps a different distance. The balance of caution and curiosity positions me outside the car barrier, but close enough to see the woman's face and the back of Pieter's head.

The woman is framed in the pavement window, level with us, hardly a metre from Pieter, eye to eye. She is oldish – old – standing quite straight in a long white robe. Her hair is awry and rather spiky; there is some remnant of makeup round the eyes and mouth. Probably because she is behind bars, the disarray looks like dementia. But she is speaking plainly to Pieter and her voice is sane.

"Not you," she says to him. "I need a *meisje* to help me. Not a man. Never you."

No thanks given for his willingness, but no rudeness either. Jolien, the nearer of us *meisjes*, steps up beside Pieter; he nods to her, bows slightly in the direction of the window and falls back.

Jolien takes the baton forward. "How can I help you?" she asks.

In reply the woman turns her back, raises her robe and, backhand, gestures at some sort of pantaloon which strains at a painful angle across her buttocks. She waits two beats, as though for dramatic effect, then, in a solemn voice, says, "It is twisted."

Jolien sees the problem: the incontinence pad needs to be hoiked up from behind, the way a child's too-baggy tights are adjusted. The woman turns and smiles encouragement, pleased to be understood. Jolien, with gentle gestures, indicates the woman's door, offers to come in and fix things.

"No need," says the woman. "We can manage through the window."

She backs herself up to the inside of the window bars and Jolien approaches close on the outside. There cannot now be more than eight inches between them.

Jolien puts her arms through the bars and grasps the dreadful undergarment in both hands. "Ready?" she asks.

"Ready," says the woman.

We hear a duet of grunts; then a triumphant "Ahhh!" Jolien now lets go and extricates herself from the bars. She steps back from the window and stands facing it. Inside, the woman does the same. A symmetrical dance. Its formality covers the shyness left by their peculiar intimacy.

The woman rescues it. "Thanks," she says briskly, lightly – as though someone had told her the time. "I hope you all have a good year."

This lets us back into the scene, breaks the spell. "You too," we say, not quite in unison. "May your wishes come true."

Breadwinner

Catherine had never been one to recognise failure. Even when the projects of her life went awry, they never went out of her control. It was a talent she had. Even as a kid she had known how to convert one kind of failure into another kind of success. And at thirty-five, with a stack of glowing job references in her rucksack, she felt capable of everything. A doctorate in refugee studies was the next career step. She knew it would be a challenge, and knew without doubt that she would rise to it. Her plan was to get through at top speed, finishing in time to settle down with a good man and have a child. There was a schedule for these things. The man she'd just left after seven amicable years didn't fit into it: he wasn't the breadwinner type. But for Catherine the break-up didn't feel like failure; more like a successful return to her proper life path.

Now in Cairo, the field study was on course. She had found a secure if bleak place to live and made good contacts among the Sudanese. The refugees were glad to tell her their stories and these became her monthly reports to base, graded 'exemplary' for the enthusiasm and efficiency they conveyed. She was enjoying the sense of moving in the right direction…

> *Omar first saw Catherine in the room at the back of the church which was the gathering place for Sudanese refugees who had made it as far as Cairo. He knew about her before this, about the American woman asking for stories about forced migration from the war zone.*
>
> *She didn't interest him. Other than news of his kin, or of sponsorships that might get him resettled, nothing was worth the effort of his attention. Nothing until that first sight of Catherine. Her head was bent close to an old man listening to him, and smiling with white teeth and a mane of dark hair. For the first time since he left his village all those months ago he felt hopeful, like one who has come out of a dark place into sunlight. He came every day to bask in it, always from a distance and without speaking. On the rare days she didn't come, he hung in a kind of limbo, staring out of the window or at the palms of his hands.*

For the best part of a week Catherine managed not to notice Omar noticing her. She told herself his looks were not remarkable: most of the men around him were equally dark-black and extremely tall; not a few threw her the same respectful, shy glances. But this one had an inward look about the eyes, and the serious quietness of him beckoned. She reminded herself that he was a potential informant, that any disturbance of personal interest would be unprofessional.

Before finally approaching him this morning she had the confusion under control, masked, at least, behind the need to collect yet another story. But his face bloomed so blatantly in front of her that her guard fell away and she was derailed by the texture of the man's skin, and his silent promise to take care of her and the children they would have.

Until now, until Omar, she hadn't been aware of need. Nothing was missing. Now, quite suddenly, looking into the radiance of his face, Catherine felt the relief of a refugee come to safety. Before Omar she hadn't felt herself to be in any sort of danger. It's true her academic supervisors had warned her of Arabs hostile to out-of-place white women and to black Africans – especially couples or groups of both. Experience proved them right; by now she was used to catcalls of abuse as she moved about the city. But she was never afraid – not even when the abuse got physical. She couldn't forget the moment when a litre or so of stinging, sticky liquid was thrown over her from a passing car; or the time two men blocked her way on the pavement while two others shoved her Sudanese companion into the line of traffic on a busy road. But until now she worried only for anyone walking with her, never for herself.

It helped that they had both been raised Roman Catholic. The priest was happy to marry them in the church and made the grand hall available afterwards. Close to two hundred people came, nearly all the present members of Omar's ethnic group. The wedding was a landmark in the community's year. True, Catherine put a chunk of her grant money into the party, but Omar's friends matched it with resources they hadn't seemed to have. Omar's ritually blessed connection with Catherine enveloped them all. And she, over the closing months of her official study period, felt herself enfolded in the collective intimacy that insiders enjoy. Living as his wife in that small, stuffy-hot room in his cousin's apartment, she came close to *knowing*. Cooking, eating, asking, listening, crying, laughing in the cramped kitchen, she learned about forced migration for the PhD, and a bit about belonging for herself.

A year after the marriage they set out for England with three-month-old Karim between them. Many people wept at the airport. Sad and happy together, Catherine thought: for them, another parting after so many, but also a chance to advance the collective hope of resettlement. And she, sad because she would be bereft of their closeness, but happy to start the future of her little family. With Karim cradled in one arm she linked the other tight with Omar's, pressing optimism into him. She smiled into his face and he nodded solemnly. They had no reason to be afraid.

Back in London, Catherine settled easily into the post-fieldwork routine, going to all the necessary seminars, meeting all the deadlines, shopping and cooking in between. They had a reasonable place to live, which Omar kept tidy while he looked after the baby, bringing him to college to collect Catherine at the end of each day. In Omar's tradition chores like these shouldn't be done by men and she tried not to notice – or to notice her colleagues noticing – how awkward he looked, a huge man in a too-small winter coat with the tiny Karim slung on his chest. It was better by the time the child had grown enough for a pushchair, but still she saw twinges of embarrassment in the friendly smiles and the calling out of greetings as the little flotilla passed. Omar, mercifully she thought, seemed not to be aware of his incongruity. He had no English when they left Cairo and wasn't talking enough to acquire any in London. Catherine didn't try to teach him; it was natural for them to speak his mother tongue together and it marked the haven of their home. English would only make distance between them. Omar was a man of few words in any language.

When he found hourly-paid work as a security guard Catherine tried to be pleased. She knew that for him the job was more important than the little money it paid, but for her it meant loss of a viable routine. There was no predictable timetable to it; he was inclined to drop everything at the shortest notice whenever he was called. He would phone Catherine to come home, and when she couldn't, would bring Karim to her. In truth she was glad of an excuse to spend time with her child, still writing in his nap intervals, or while he played with scrap printer paper on the carpeted floor.

Catherine's grant had a year to run when they came back to London. She began to plan for the post-grant period, expecting to finish on time and slide seamlessly into a new source of decent family income. She applied and was accepted for a plum job in the USA, due to start as soon as she had the PhD. Omar told her he was happy about this; he had come to believe that his new life was on hold in England, that it could only take off in the New World. In America he would learn English, finish his education, get a good job, be a proper man again… He said it aloud: "As soon as you finish that paper," he told her, "I'll be able to do good things."

In the autumn of this final year Karim fell ill with a virus picked up in his nursery group. A month of anxiety and hospital visits threw Catherine off schedule. As soon as Karim was better, Omar got sick, probably with the same thing, and lost the connection with the security firm that employed him. He wasn't really ill for long, but remained morose and unhelpful. Catherine could see why he was unwilling – maybe unable – to expose himself to the failure of not getting, or of getting, another nothing job. She told herself his heaviness would pass.

But it did not, and by the end of the year she fell into a dreadful fatigue. Perhaps it wasn't just extra domestic burdens which caused the December miscarriage, but they certainly slowed her recovery from it. She knew the loss saddened Omar too; they had planned a sibling for Karim, close enough in age to be his companion and soon enough to make the family ready for its new life. Now it seemed that wouldn't happen either. The Americans sent a letter to tell her, *with regret*, that the deadline to take up that perfect appointment could not be extended. In the same week, her grant ran out and she took a meagre temporary job in college administration, covering someone's maternity leave.

The small flat that had been a haven was suddenly only small. And cold; they burned the gas fire in short bursts to save money and Omar was not as warm toward her as before. Nor, she knew, was she towards him. Each evening, once they had eaten and Karim was asleep in his alcove behind the Mickey Mouse curtain, Catherine cleared the all-purpose table for her computer and papers and tried to write. Omar sat close to her; there was no room not to. When he did talk it was usually to ask her when she'd be finished – when tonight, when the thesis? Mostly he rustled the newspaper he was pretending to read and sighed a lot. She could not blank out the sound or her resentment of it. She began to be afraid.

This morning the eagerness on his son's face jolts Omar out of the dark space he has been living in. He sees the resemblance and remembers his first sight of Catherine, that same punch of sunlight. He bundles the toddler up against the awful cold of London, straps him tidily into the pushchair and sets out to walk the streets. Perhaps he will find something out there. Even if no solution comes to him, at least Karim will be excited to see people and cars and dogs. Omar manoeuvres down the narrow hall to the outside door, past the shopping trolley of one neighbour and the bicycle of another, careful not to scrape anything, making sure Karim's mittened hands are on board before stepping into the heavy chill of the London winter.

The road is empty, nothing in sight that isn't grey. Karim's eagerness has faded and he hunches low in his pushchair. Omar has lost the mood that got him started; he keeps on toward the High Street only because going forward must be better than going back home. As they turn the corner Omar sees, halfway up, on the opposite side, a blaze of yellow. He crouches down and points it out to Karim, who begins to squeal and bounce up and down against the strap of the pram. They cross at the zebra and speed up to get nearer. It is balloons. Outside the high glass door a man is holding a bunch of yellow balloons.

The man smiles and gives one to Karim. He shakes Omar's hand and makes a shivering gesture in reference to the cold. Omar finds him friendly and doesn't move away; the man asks him how long they have lived in London, whether he and his fine family enjoyed their first English Christmas.

Omar, tongue-tied by shyness, mumbles, "One year" and "Yes" and then stands silent, stooping slightly to compensate for the other's lack of height. The man steps closer and places his hand behind Omar's arm, drawing him gently forward.

"I don't know about you," he says in a quiet voice, the way a friend tells a secret, "but I always find the Christmas season very expensive. And after Christmas a man needs extra cash to buy the things his family should have…"

Omar nods agreement. He gropes for words to tell the man that he too is a good husband and father; that he too wants to give his wife and son the things they want. That he too never has enough to do it right. It is a relief to say these things out loud.

Now it's the man's turn to nod. "I can tell you how to fix it," he says. "There is a way to get cash, even today, to pay debts, to buy good things. You can borrow some money from this bank. Everyone does it," he says. "That's what we are here for…"

Omar understands lending; a person will give what he has to the one who needs it because he trusts they will return the favour when they can. Gradually the miracle flows over him. The man trusts me. His bank will give me money so that we can live until Catherine finishes and our new life begins, and I can get good work and give it back. Karim waves his balloon and crows. The nice man, still smiling, holds the door for the pushchair, leads them to a table called 'Private Banker' and introduces Omar – he gets the name exactly right – to the man sitting behind it.

"This gentleman would like a personal loan of £5,000," he tells him. "Please arrange it for him."

"Certainly," says the colleague. "May I get you a cup of tea? Can your handsome son have a biscuit? Just sign the two forms on the line. See; I have marked the place."

Omar has been feeling light and strong all afternoon. He has shopped for food with money drawn from the new account and has a fine meal ready to surprise Catherine.

It is weeks since he made food. Maybe she will wonder what's happened and will ask about it when she's settled a bit and is not so tired. Maybe when they've eaten… But Omar can't contain his pride.

"Look at this," he says. "I have something for you." He spreads the loan agreement out on their one table, pushing the ready supper dishes aside and leaning close over her shoulder to point out the bank's logo, the impressive sums, his own signature. "Now you can finish," he says to her. "Now we can be happy again…"

Omar doesn't understand why Catherine looks away from him and starts to cry. He doesn't understand why she won't stop crying.

Elephant in the Room

Our butcher is twins. Identical. Originally, that is. You wouldn't know it from their names: Ted and Oliver, known as Olly. I wonder what their parents were thinking. Most often, faced with two peas in a pod, people go cute. Ted and Fred, maybe. Oliver and Alistair.

The business was built on the trade of Bloomsbury residents and restaurants, but now its reputation has spread to include non-locals from all over London. Those who cannot fit into the small, sawdusted shop chat cheerfully out on the pavement, waiting for one to come out so that one can go in. It's hard to know who's there for the banter and who for the sausages. Ted and Olly are the source of both; meat-buyers often speak of "dropping in on the twins". Customers get used to their mirror likeness. In the dim, bluish light they could look like two versions of one man behind the high glass counter.

I can't remember when this began to change. But suddenly, shockingly, it struck us that the face of one twin was drawn and yellow, his eyes sunken, his voice subdued. Olly was ill. More and more there was only one twin behind the counter. It was always Ted. He built an Olly bulletin into his banter, but kept it cheerful. When well-meaning customers empathised with dreary stories of other people's tumours, chemo, hair loss, distress, he would deflect them into discussion of spicy sausage or today's best lamb. Somehow, though, not talking about Olly only made it worse. The line outside got shorter.

And then Ted put up a sign inviting sponsors for his London Marathon run. The relief was wonderful. Now we could banter about training regimes – which shoes, which diet, how many miles – tease Ted about his paunch, and then about the shrinking of it. The lines outside grew back. Olly still wasn't around of course, but now his absence and his cancer could be acknowledged. The elephant left the room.

Ted finished the distance. Not fast, but triumphant, his *I'm running for Olly* banner held up to the end. Next morning at the shop it was as if he'd scored the winning goal for England. Only he wasn't there. "Wrecked" was the message passed on by the cashier. He did appear two days later, limping discreetly, modestly proud. And amazingly, visiting the shop to say thank you, there too was Olly, similarly unsteady, equally proud.

We cheer them both. And for a minute the gloss of celebration masks what we all see: the twins are not identical anymore. Olly and Ted are wrecked in different ways.

Listening for Water

His habit, and eventually ours, was not to draw attention to any of this. It was as if we'd agreed a kind of truce among us so we didn't have to notice he was peculiar. If visitors asked about it we only shrugged. "That's how he *is*, we would say; he listens for water…"

As the years passed it got worse. Just after the war, when we were children and he was still a reasonably young man, it was only brushing your teeth with the tap running that riled him. Lots of dads felt like that at the time. Water *costs*, they all said; always the same story. Our dad started like them but gradually he moved into a different league. Now any unaccounted water noise set him off. He'd look up from his paper, stop talking mid-sentence, stop chewing mid-chew to listen, turning his head and his eyes towards the sound. The fainter it was, the sharper he felt it. Any distant drip was worse than a torrent.

"There's water running," he'd say – as if we hadn't heard it – half rising from the chair when it started, letting go his breath to sit down again if it stopped; setting off to find the source if it didn't.

In the good, early years of his retirement, Pa kept a stock of tap washers and a range of wrenches in the study, next to his old medical bag, telling himself and the rest of us that he was still a doctor, only now it was taps. Our dad the tap doctor. If a neighbour so much as hinted at water trouble he'd be over there with his tools, making house calls like the old days. "For sheer satisfaction," he used to say, "there's nothing like stopping a drip."

But even he couldn't fix what wasn't there. More and more often, as he got old, we saw him react to sounds that only he could hear. Out of nothing he would raise his hand, palm forward and up, demanding silence as he strained to situate the drip-drop-dripping noise buried somewhere in his head.

When war started in 1939 he had a medical practice in a not-so-good part of Central London. Could have done better for himself, they said: clever, personable, well-qualified. Harley Street material, according to his wife, no doubt referring to herself. But he couldn't be comfortable with privilege and was careless of patients' ability to pay the proper money for his services. He was content with pickles, home-grown vegetables; carpentry work. Topped up by a handful of wealthy clients it was enough to get by.

Early in 1940 he arranged for Mum to take us kids to Canada. On the dock he told us he was happy because we'd be safe; the Blitz soon came to structure his time. He would sleep through the bombing, waking when it stopped, groping his way through the still-dark streets to join the Heavy Rescue volunteers. Their job was to release the living from the rubble of bombed buildings; his was to impose a kind of triage, deciding whether survivors needed only sweet tea and a bandage, or blood transfusions and surgery. He relished a buoyancy of common purpose with the rescue teams, and the dogged humour-in-adversity of the people they rescued. Those nine months of the Blitz were for him the best of times: all in it together, everyone equal.

In May of 1941 the German planes moved off to Russia and the war settled into its steady grind. Now there was nothing for it but to become an army doctor. He went straight in as principal medical officer over British Somaliland and its newly surrendered, UK-administered Italian counterpart. In Mogadishu the army set him up in a splendid castellated house with marble floors, a sunken bath, two house servants and an Abyssinian cook.

He learnt that his authority in the job depended on toeing the lines of local order; that privilege let him do what had to be done. Two ex-pat Italian enterprises were suspended as threats to public health: until he came, children working in the match factory inhaled the fumes of sulphur; the local ice cream was made with TB-contaminated milk. And, of course, medical standards had to be optimal. Poor infrastructure, staff and medicine shortages and regular drought were limiting factors, not excuses. The main hospital had not been so efficient for decades, and he made regular inspections of the small field hospitals scattered three or four days' journey from the capital.

Twice a year he set off on safari with two Land Rovers – one for stores and drinking water; the other for an Italian factotum who could make maps, speak Swahili, shoot game and play backgammon, and a retinue of Africans, each with a designated role in the journey's process. The medical orderly was plainly top among the Africans, trapped in a buffer zone between black and white. Next came the two drivers, the cook and the man who prepared the *bwana*'s clothes and shaving water.

Below these was a generalised set of three whose duty it was to set the *bwana*'s tent at dusk and take it down at dawn, and to collect wood for the cook's fire and the all-night blaze. These three negotiated their own power structure. The youngest was bottom. First to carry, last to speak. He slept only in the lurching Land Rover when the group was on the road. At night he was the watchman, staying upright and awake to feed the fire and guard against the circle of hyenas encroaching in the dark. The fire kept them back a steady distance. It shone pink in their eyes.

We always nagged at our dad to tell us safari stories. The hyenas were best, but he could make your eyes bulge with images of wild game and swamp snakes and the hot, pale desert. Your skin went dry with the longing for water to wash with. Your stomach would clench for the bleeding *dik-dik*, just shot for supper, its belly steaming while the cook cleaned away its innards…

We loved his stories. He had been so good at telling them that now, every time he refused, we felt the loss – an old man who mostly stares out over the flowerbeds and waits for teatime is no big attraction. Except quite often he gave you the feeling he was remembering something so terrible he couldn't bring himself to talk about it. Of course we probed: worse than pink-eyed hyenas with blotchy, ratty fur and piggy feet must be a story worth hearing!

But he would only shake his head and look away: "Eat another biscuit. There is nothing more for you to know."

I had been away travelling when they moved him to the hospice, and now I went to visit him whenever I could. Already I missed what he used to be. How would I feel when nothing of him was there? On that last day the room was full of cards and photos and all the final signs of admiration and affection, of a life well lived. He asked to go into the garden. Outside he rested quietly in his wheelchair and I sat on the bench beside him, wondering about death. The garden was shrill with yellow flowers.

Quite suddenly he sat straight and turned towards me, alert with the effort. "I need to tell you something," he said. "I've kept it quiet so long. I haven't had words. But now I want you to know it."

I smiled, glad he felt like another story, but his face was bleak.

"It runs behind my eyes like a loop of film, round and round. I watch it like a newsreel, like someone who wasn't there. But I *was* there. That's the pity of it. There's the shame." He stopped and looked down at his hands.

After a while I asked him if this thing, this film in his head, had to do with water.

He shrugged. "I used to think so. I used to believe that if I could stop the dripping and the wasting the shame would go away. Such foolishness! How could anything in this life make that happen? Truth is, shame has stained even the things I did well." He was quiet again. A bumblebee made the only sound.

"Tell me the film," I said. He closed his eyes and looked away. When at last he spoke, it was as if I wasn't there…

It is the end of the day's driving. The Land Rovers are parked for the night, one behind the other, forming a short wall against the bush. The drivers tinker under the raised bonnet of one of them. A circle of ground has been cleared for camp, the fire is rising and the bwana*'s tent is up. His valet person sets a basin of clear water on the canvas wash stand, a piece of soap in the soap niche and a clean towel on the chair. The* bwana *hands over his road-dusty shirt and stands bare for his wash. He soaps his hands, splashes water over his face, neck and chest, then sinks his arms elbow-deep in the basin, up and down a few times. He dries himself on the towel and slides into the crisp khaki shirt held up for him. He nods thanks for it and calls out a teasing greeting to the cook. The general mood lifts.*

The Italian factotum repeats the washing sequence – same water, same towel, only marginally less deference. Next in line, the medical orderly lifts the basin off the wash stand, carries it carefully across the clearing and sets it on the flat bonnet of the second Land Rover. He flicks his hands in the water and wipes them through his hair. The cook follows – a similar rinse, but drying instead on the cloth tucked apron-like into the top of his trousers. The drivers wave away their turn: they must fix the sick vehicle before dark, and anyway, it will be too cold to be wet once the sun is gone.

It is setting as the unskilled trio returns from the bush. Each of the two older men holds a knotted sackcloth of firewood over one shoulder and the machete used to chop it in his free hand. The youngster carries a load no bigger than the adults', but for him it is heavier. He walks a distance behind them, dragging his burden along the ground. By the time he gets it to the fire site the others have stoked the flame and are resting on their haunches beside it.

The boy hovers about, not settling. He glances at the basin on the Land Rover – once, twice, again. Much of the water has been splashed away. What's left is coloured russet by the laterite the others have washed off. Soap film on its surface glints metallic in the fading light. The boy asks whether the water is finished with. Yes, yes. No one pays him attention. He walks across the clearing, wiping his dry mouth with the back of his fist. Now he grasps the bowl in both hands and drinks it dry. The dregs of water gulp noisily down his throat. Slaked now, and silent, he joins the others at the fireside.

The film stopped there. The buzz saw of the bumblebee rose louder between us, but nothing could cover the terrible soft sound of my father weeping.

Pa's Chair

When we were children it was even bigger. It has a back shaped like a shield, padded arms sticking straight out; thick, squashy cushion for the seat. Below, the base is solid iron, medieval, with a heavy corkscrew to change the height and a wheel knob to secure it, all locked into a solid X with casters on the feet like metal oranges. Its brown leather skin used to smell nicely of dog. These days, wax is what I conjure.

When we were children it was Pa's working place. He sat behind his desk to talk to patients, leaning back into the chair's tilt to listen. Sometimes he'd swivel right round to take a book off the shelf; other times, when he needed a stethoscope or to look closer at a person, he would twirl exactly the quarter necessary to free his knees and stand up. My brother and I marvelled at his mastery.

By the time Pa died my brother was pretty much a recluse. He told me relationships used him up, and that relationships with our parents encroached more than any. Even so, he made a special effort when we knew Pa was fading. I was allowed to book and buy a plane ticket so they could see each other before the end, but Pa was

gone the day before he was due to fly. My brother didn't
manage the funeral.

I guess the lack of completion left a space in him.
While at first he wanted none of the pieces bequeathed
to us from Pa's flat, when the small shipment finally
arrived he changed his mind and took the chair. It stayed
with him for a handful of years. For a while he seemed
able to control its encroachment by neglect; mostly it
sat turned to the wall, its skin drying and cracking, its
cushion bleeding the ancient feathers that stuffed it.
Eventually – I never knew the catalyst – my brother
announced that he planned to change his life, redo his
flat; that the chair was to be thrown away.

We rescued it, of course, wrestling it down the three
flights of his stairs and into our car. The hatch door had
to be left open. I was like a child again, dwarfed by the
size and weight of the thing. At the other end it didn't
fit round the narrow corner of our entrance hall. Good
that we now had no need to struggle it up more stairs
and stack things to make space once we got there. Not so
good that the chair now sat half-wedged in the corridor,
crooked but dignified, demanding a solution.

A nice restoration man released the blockage after a long
four days. He rolled the chair noisily as far as his van;
he'd parked it on the double yellow with flashing lights to
signal serious cargo. But then three of us were needed to
hoist it aboard. As Pa's chair moved off, upright this time,
I confess to extra relief at the prospect of not seeing it for
a while. At last it would be tended, but not straight away.

As things worked out, the nice man had it with him longer than any of us expected. His wife was found to have breast cancer, was treated, was depressed, rejected him. But in the fullness of time he turned back to Pa's chair, oiled its metal parts, patched its rigid arms, made a new seat cushion with a velvet cover almost the brown of the old leather back, and bandaged it with wide plastic strips. The loading procedure of its going away was reversed for the return, except that now the owner of the empty shop downstairs had been persuaded that Pa's chair would make his space look less abandoned and more attractive to tenants.

But before that could happen, a marvellous coincidence resolved everything. While the chair was away our daughter's man, Pa's grandson-in-law, had added a vast extension to the back of their house. Now that it was finished they felt the size of it more a bleakness than a convenience. The sight of Pa's chair in solitary splendour in the middle of an empty room, warming it like an open hearth, convinced them of the chair's rightful belonging.

So Pa's chair came home. For the grandson-in-law it is a haven for his after work recovery. The great-grandson sees it as we did when we were children, although with a less distant respect for his father and the chairs he sits in. Pa's chair for him is a dreaming place. He doesn't yet have a shelf of books to refer to or a line of patients to cure. But it's already clear he has the lean-back-full-twirl-quarter-turn talent in his genes.

Redemption

For eight years now he had carried another man's name. He needed to get out of there and into here and all it took was a different name: Michael P instead of George Q. It was easy enough to do at the time: the right balance of money and menace makes a travel document. It's the living with it since that's been hard. Not fear anymore, but a kind of shame. During five of the eight years he punished the he that wasn't him with drugs, graduating up to heroin, until he hit a new bottom and feared that, whoever he was, he would die. Nine months of painful effort later he came out clean, a birthling swaddled in the messages of counselling: *Redemption is possible. Mistakes can be rectified. Happier endings can happen…* This mantra keeps him clear of everything except the lie.

Without drugs to cover it he tries for the white noise of too much work. He's a short order cook in a greasy spoon restaurant. Works every day, all the hours they will give him. It feels like someone else's job, but it's good to be in control, even of a rubbish meal, start to finish, each task rounded off before the next one is started. If only his clothes, his very self (whichever self…) didn't stink of grease and the rest of it. Someone else's clothes. Someone else's skin.

Home after every shift, he shuts the clothes in the machine and takes a long, hot shower to wash away the stench of food and failure. Every day. He stays under the water till it starts to run cold, then lets the clothes have it. The shower needs to be hot, the soap where it should be, a dry mat on the floor, the towel clean enough. Every day. Slough it off. Begin again. Clean clothes, skin out.

Michael-*cum*-George was married once. As good as. She stood by him through the addiction but threw him out for 'moodiness' fifteen months back. She doesn't know who he is. Or isn't. He was glad to leave really. Except for Charlie. They see each other maybe once in two months, but the joy's going out of it: the kid knows his dad's not straight with him but he doesn't know what's crooked.

There's been no woman in his life since. How could there be? What would he tell her? Anyway, he's afraid of any situation that might get complicated, more complicated, before it can come right. He does have one friend left over from the recovery days. He hadn't intended friendship, but halfway through recovery he lost control, let his guard down like you're supposed to, and told Terry about the lie. Whatever it is between them has blossomed, in spite of both of them, into a kind of trust. Terry knows about the lie and he, for his part, knows he knows. When things are going well it's good to talk on the phone every so often, gossiping about acquaintances who have slipped, each reassured by the other's steadiness. So Terry was the first to hear him thinking aloud about applying for citizenship.

"I've been here long enough now, Tel. Maybe I should travel, go and see my family. Imagine having a passport! Charlie could be proud of a dad with a passport. Not just a rubbish migrant; a proper British citizen. Even his mum might soften up to me for that. Maybe we'll start again as a proper family. What d'you think Tel?"

Terry has learned to be cautious, low risk in all things. He has his own problems and sometimes these calls set him back. But it's good this time to hear optimism instead of the usual gloom. Says, "Why not?" Maybe a passport will bring the poor sod out of his shell, put him back on the up, open his horizons. Neither of them says anything about the lie.

Phone calls later, heart pounding, Michael-once-George posts off an application to be British. This second time of asking for someone else's identity should be easier than the first, but it isn't. The official letter that comes back brings the threat of discovery on to his doormat, thinly veiled in bureaucratic prose, revealed by *the time necessary to process each case*. His anxiety builds as the weeks pass, seeping through the frenzy of work and leeching the trust out of friendship. Terry dreads the now-daily call. Always the same themes.

"They'll find out. I'll be deported. I'll lose Charlie. I can't sleep. The job stinks. My life is shit. What if I start using again?" And every time: "You should have stopped me, Tel."

Terry is sorry enough for the poor bugger, but he got

himself into it, didn't he? The way the guy wails down the phone makes him so angry sometimes that he has to shout at him, to defend himself from the contagion of dread and hope that could derail them both. One day, weeks into it and still no ruling on the case, his own problems mounting, Terry loses his rag altogether. Tells him to give it a rest.

"Just *be* Michael, for fuck's sake. It'll be *your* passport, *your* ugly face on it. Or tell them you're sorry, you made a mistake, you're really George, and please can they send you home and not to jail. Do *something.* And listen. Stop phoning me. I can't take any more…"

The man who used to be George hits bottom for the second time, knowing, for the second time, that if he doesn't change he – whoever he is – will die. He stays in his room for a week, barely eating, not washing, sleeping only to have terrible dreams, haunted awake by demons. And then, like the other cold turkey, the hell lets him go. He lands in the silence that follows a police siren in the night, and a kind of conviction begins to fill it. *Redemption is possible. Mistakes can be rectified. Happier endings can happen.*

He showers hot and long, shaves, puts on fresh clothes, clears and cleans the chaos of the table and sits down to write the letter. Tells them he has a passport application pending, reference number blah blah, that he still wants to be, *would* be, a good British citizen. But he needs to tell them that he made the application under a false name. That he is George Q, not Michael P. That everything else on the form is true. That he is sorry for their trouble but the reasons are complicated. And that… That's all. Yours sincerely.

The weight of the address slows his hand as he writes it, and it sets the pace of the actions which follow: folding the letter into the envelope, licking it closed, finding a stamp, walking to the corner postbox – all slow motion unreal. He watches himself doing it like someone else's performance. Back at work the next day he does his stuff with the food and picks up the bathing/laundering ritual when he gets home, but still as an observer. Through the coming days he feels liminal, waiting between names, between here, where he is, and there, where they'll send him. Quite calm now. Workmates remark on it. Has something happened?

With a distant smile he says, "No, but soon it will."

And finally it does. One night, along with two Oxfam circulars, a pizza voucher and a gas bill, the stiff manila envelope is on the mat, sent first class to Mr George Q. It must belong to someone else: nobody has written to his mother's son in all these years. Not known at this address. He stares at the words *Free Pizza Delivery*, mouthing them silently until his mind clears and lets him remember what the letter means. It means it's over. His heart gets fast and louder as he stacks the post, carries it in two hands to the table and places it squarely in front of the chair where he will sit. Slowly and carefully he reads the gas bill, the pizza voucher, the Oxfam circulars. And then the letter. And again…

"Listen to me, Tel. Don't hang up. This will blow you away. Something wonderful. You know I sent the letter to say I wasn't who I said? Yes. Weeks and weeks ago when you told me. The lie was killing me, Tel. You know how it is. Even if they sent me back I was ready to go, leaving Charlie, everything. Then comes this crazy answer. Can it be a joke? It says a passport is on its way to me. To the George me! Honest to God, Tel!"

Terry is stunned for a moment, then cursing, laughing, crying with his friend. He shouts, this time in jubilation. This time, this one time, it's come good like they promised.

One time is all it takes.

The Healer

This, Child, is how it will be.

You will know before others see it that you are different. The difference will become plain to them only after your journey. It will happen quite soon; this illness of your eyes is the beginning. When you come back you will not remember where you have been or what you saw. You will not believe how long you were away until the growth of your body and the lines on my face tell you the time.

When you come back you will know things that others cannot imagine. Some of them I will tell you. Even when you are not with me I will tell you things. Some you will learn from spirits whose voices even I will not hear. Your spirits will come as they are ready, one at a time, each with a name and a voice that is theirs always, only for you. You will know which one to call for the special understanding of each thing that is asked of you.

They will never leave you; you will never be alone. They will be the ones to say what work you may not do in the house, who will decide whether you should carry water or dig the garden. While you are still a child your father and your mother will grow angry and call you disobedient, but you will not heed them; you will know that the spirits will make them ill or they will make you lame if they are disobeyed. And when you are fully grown they will be ready to block from you the sounds of the life that others enjoy, and to keep you from the ordinary ways of a good woman.

Your neighbours will realise that you are not like them; always you will be on the outside. They will say they cannot let you close because they fear you, and you will learn that you can only help them if you remain apart. In this way the people around you will seem to echo the spirit voices. If you marry, your husband will tell you to choose and you will not and he will leave you; if you bear children they will go from you; if you attend the church the priest will tell you to renounce the voices and you will not heed him. You will never have the chance to be like others.

I know how hard it will be, Child. I know that life. The spirits have chosen you to be their instrument and their power is a gift that cannot be refused. But be comforted: by claiming you they have made themselves your instruments. From now forever your spirits will be there when you call them up. They have given you a gift that will never be taken away. You will use their powers in your work, but it will be your name, not theirs, that others will call when they need help – when they have lost some precious thing; when their brother raves and threatens; when there is a sickness in their hearts or limbs; when a child or a wife is wasting away; when a husband is straying. Even without touching you will know what kind of suffering they have and which of your spirits should be called. That spirit will tell you what herbs to use, what actions and treatments to perform, and what you must tell your patient to do or to change. You will speak to them in your own voice: your patients will never hear the voices that you hear.

This gift will not make you rich in money; even a person with nothing cannot be turned away. Most will bring a small thing to open the bag of possibility and will try to pay something later. When their problem is cured they will praise your spirits' power and even people far from these villages will respect you for it. They will not let you be hungry; they will help you with heavy work; they will protect you from storms and vandals – and they will keep you apart.

You will stay always in this compound, outside the ordinary life of the village. As I have done. But you will never be alone. Your spirits will be your company. They will never leave you. You are chosen.

I tell you these things, Child, just as my grandfather told me; just as you will tell another in your turn.

Peggy's Choices

The family photo posed in the year she turned fourteen shows Peggy back row centre, between Violet and Winnie. The older sisters' face outward at a slight angle, smiling a little, focusing on the middle distance. Peggy, in contrast, stands unsmiling, four-square to the camera, looking so directly into it that the viewer doesn't doubt her claim to be the focus of the picture.

In the row in front, their parents sit straight and stiff on hard chairs. They are fashionably dressed and look modestly pleased with themselves. Charlotte – usually Lottie – has her hair swept up in a roll which adds a fat two inches to her height, bringing her close to Albert's level. He sits to her left, cross-legged; the full skirt of Lottie's frock encroaches delicately over his thigh.

The boys are placed either side of the grown-ups and look gravely into the camera. Ernie, who is eight, sits on a stool to the right of the picture with his legs crossed exactly like his father's. Len, on the left, is a couple of years younger and has nothing to sit on. The best he can do is cross his ankles, achieving something like a manly stance by leaning a shoulder against the wall.

This is the family presenting itself; like Len's pose, it's the best they can do. It doesn't change the reality of penny-pinching or Lottie's taste for the gin, but the effort of respectability shines through like respectability proper. Even those who know better are convinced by it. They gather round the print after Sunday tea – "Ernie touched it, Dad." "I did not." "Leave off with your jammy fingers, Len" – and each, looking at it, is proud of the person they would like to be.

While the others marvel at themselves, Peggy pretends to clear the tea things in the kitchen.

If she looks at the portrait she sees only the mismatch between who she is and who she should be. Now, choosing not to cry, she strikes viciously at the tap, running the water hard enough to splash the floor. *One day I'll make the pieces fit.*

Four years later the portrait, nicely framed, keeps pride of place on the mantelpiece: a piece of furniture among the rest. Peggy still expects to emerge into her proper self, but has yet to find out who that will be. She has become a stunner. Not pretty, exactly – too much nose bridge; not enough lower lip – but with eyes that flash green and blue, slim ankles and high breasts, easy to laugh and cry. The pay-attention-to-me directness that put people off her as a sturdy teenager counts as personality in this new version; now she has 'it'. The lads buzz around her. So far none has claimed the prize. Never mind; the combination of vitality and general flirtiness holds them hopeful.

The first time Cecil sees her, strolling with her friends in the park, giggling together, whispering behind their hands, he too is in thrall. Peggy is outside his world; quite suddenly he wants to be there with her.

Cecil is in his late twenties, a medical intern exhausted by the effort of graduating. His parents' ambition for him remains firm: within the year a new brass plate, *Cecil Siggs MD*, will hang below his father's (*Richard Siggs MD, MRCP*) and the assisted climb towards partnership in the family practice will begin. Richard Siggs is not much impressed by his son, but fond enough, not openly critical, confident that Cecil will shape up in time. He can be sure his wife Rosemary – not Rose, never Rosie – will keep the boy on track, managing him along with the housemaid, the cook, the gardener and the family's social calendar. Today, while their son walks the fateful shortcut that crosses his path with Peggy's, Rosemary sits at the polished wood escritoire in her sewing room to compile a list of the eligible daughters among her acquaintance. According to plan, Cecil will choose one of them and begin his professional life as a married man.

Until this moment Cecil has had no experience of girls or women, let alone of flirts or people of the 'other' class. Studying has filled his time and the family has fenced his life. Of course he is naïve, and of course, outside home ground, he doesn't know how to behave. Peggy notices him hovering but she is used to causing a stir, and anyway, a quick glance confirms that this man is not interesting. Tall, certainly, but angular and awkward, with glasses glinting in the sun, a too-dark suit and hair combed straight back like an undertaker.

But obsession drives him nearer and the girls become curious enough to let him catch up. Once level with them and finally close to Peggy, he gropes for something to say. The bell of the cart selling ice cream saves him.

"Would you ladies permit me to buy you each an ice?"

There is a flurry of choosing flavours and changing minds. Cecil is patient and courteous with them all, approving their choices, commenting on the weather, asking if they walk here often... This is plainly a respectful and respectable person. Peggy surveys him through her excellent lashes as she licks her ice. His suit is lovely cloth and tailor-made; the glasses are gold-rimmed; he paid for the ices with a pound note instead of coins; he offered cigarettes from a flat silver case... He begins to look attractive.

Their courtship progresses slowly and sedately through the summer. In the early days they meet only in the park, and always in the company of some number of Peggy's girlfriends. They walk there on Sundays and Thursdays; Sunday, of course, is free of work and Thursday's early closing gives them the afternoon off. Peggy works for a dressmaker who lets her model for the customers, and sometimes borrow 'the latest' to wear for a special occasion.

So twice a week Cecil finds and follows the little group like a faithful hound, eager to buy ices without number if this will ensure access to his lady. A few weeks in, he musters the courage to invite Peggy – alone – to tea. She is quite ready for this – a swathed skirt, a borrowed blouse with ruffles at the neck, a short, body-hugging jacket – and their entrance into the Savoy lounge causes the mild sensation she has come to expect. Going down the carpeted steps she rests her hand lightly on Cecil's arm.

She has been thinking about him rather a lot. By now she feels a sort of comfort in his presence, but, being honest, little else. True, she has begun cautiously to imagine a future on his arm, in his lovely house, which she has yet to see, in his bed… But the thought stops there: he has strong hands and clean fingernails and a nice, crisp, Cologne-y smell, but, flirting aside, she knows too little about sex to recognise what might or might not be signs of a satisfactory lover. It is enough to be taken to an elegant tearoom with a white cloth on the table, tiny lace napkins, proper cutlery and attentive waitresses with starched aprons. The cake stand is three tiers high, with different dainty items on each layer. It nudges a memory of the bread slices on the meat platter at home, and Peggy has a back-rush of feeling that makes her want to weep. Cecil is half right in imagining it is gratitude to him that moistens her eyes.

This is the first of many outings alone together – first teas, then suppers; a couple of concerts. Always their behaviour is circumspect: smiles exchanged when they meet, a furtive kiss on her cheek when they part; once he held her hand crossing the road. There is nothing of prurient interest to tell the other girls. She plays down the luxury of it all so as not to upset them.

If she ignores the fact that Cecil never invites her to his home, puts her on the bus, once into a taxi, but never offers to take her to her door – anyway she wouldn't let him go inside it – she is increasingly confident of his attachment and of her influence. The influence goes both ways: he has exposed her to moneyed places and classical music – even a new name; he told her one evening, much to her delight, that he will call her Diana because Peggy does no justice to her beauty. But her effects on him are more concrete: he has combed his hair to the side since she said it would make him look 'dashing', and the infection of her vitality shows in the length and speed of his stride.

At first Rosemary is not alarmed. Knowing her son, she expects whatever he is going through will pass in a week or so, like a summer cold. She watches him narrowly of course, but with no more than cautious interest – until she sees him pausing to check himself in the hall mirror as he leaves the house. Something like anxiety takes hold. It stays with her all day.

When she hears Cecil's key in the door that evening she summons him to her sewing room and quizzes him about his movements, his friends, his availability for gatherings at which he will meet the three or four young women she has identified as eligible wife material. This first time his responses are non-committal but cheerful. *Hasn't he just had tea with Peggy?* He tells Rosemary there is nothing to worry about. She is not reassured: a good mother doesn't let such matters drop; grown boys with prospects must be monitored, deterred from bad habits, protected from wrong women.

As days pass her momentum builds. Cecil becomes more evasive, more often out for meals that he claims to eat with medical colleagues, less present when he is at home, less responsive, less – Richard agrees – less like himself.

So much is he not himself that, quite alone, he comes to his own conclusion. The situation is intolerable: he senses himself splayed between Peggy and his parents, knowing at the same time that his feelings for her and his dependency on them are set equally hard in his bones. The solution is plain and simple: he must bring them together. His mother will see that Peggy is right for him; Peggy will see that he and his family are right for her. He will marry Peggy and bring her to live with him in his parents' home.

At his next meeting with her Cecil conveys the first step in this sequence to Peggy, but not the second. He tells her that his mother wants them to come to tea this coming Sunday, but says nothing about his marriage plans. Nor does he report the context of Rosemary's invitation. Telling him yet again of the charms of her dear friend Mrs E's daughter, she had been surprised but pleased to hear him agree that "Yes, it is time for me to marry." But then an 'and'…

"And what?" The pause has raised her alarm.

"And," he says, "I have found the woman I want for my wife."

There follows a new line of quizzing – "Who is she? What of her family? Do I know them? Where did you meet?"

Holding fast to the shreds of his resolution, Cecil tells his mother that he wants them to meet, that he knows she will support his choice. Rosemary is mollified; he is still enough himself to need her approval.

So Peggy arrives at the tea party without knowing that Cecil has decided to marry her, or that his mother, and therefore his father, vigorously oppose the plan. Not knowing of any reason to be nervous, she is, on this first meeting, radiant with self–assurance. Rosemary is warily impressed, and also by the elegant understatement of Peggy's clothes. Looking her over – the eyes, the neatly bobbed hair, the discreetly fitted jacket – she is reassured by a half-memory of seeing her somewhere before. Richard's enchantment is complete, although complicated by shadows of pride and envy. Cecil has small twinges of unfocused anxiety in the beginning, but fewer as the afternoon progresses. He need not have worried; our Peggy, introduced as Diana, knows how to behave. The pretensions of Lottie and Albert here stand her in good stead.

The havoc begins when Rosemary wakes in the night remembering where she has in fact seen Peggy before: not at church, not in a gallery or at the coming out of somebody's daughter, but in that shabby dressmaker's shop where she went, not to buy clothes, of course, but to get the dining room curtains hemmed on the cheap. She rouses Richard with the shrill news that Cecil's intended is a common shop girl. Hazy with sleep, Richard is not surprised; he always knew his son for the kind of fool to be caught by a wily tart. Great catch indeed! He turns to the wall and Rosemary's tirade fades into dreams of his own youth.

By the time Cecil comes down to breakfast Rosemary has composed herself, but her eyes are icy and her lips so exceptionally tight that he feels again like a small boy whose present to his mother is rejected. Once he painted a picture for her birthday and she threw it in the bin; this time he offered his lovely Peggy. Their meeting has fixed nothing.

As soon as the housemaid bringing new coffee has left the room Rosemary lets go her composure and attacks him with a volley of staccato exclamations: "Why do you lie? This won't do! It's got to stop! Who is she anyway? Little slut! I suppose she's pregnant!"

This last provokes a denial, a mumble about waiting to be married.

"Good," says Rosemary. "That makes it easier to send her packing!"

Cecil stays silent, buttering a piece of toast with every sign of acquiescence. Apparently satisfied, his mother dabs her napkin to the corners of her mouth, pushes back from the table and leaves the room to begin organising her resources. Cecil continues to chew, slowly and thoughtfully. He savours a new and powerful sense of contrary resolve: he will keep her; he will marry her; he will make his mother receive her as his wife. He eats his breakfast with good appetite and leaves the house.

And what of Peggy? First, of course, she needs to agree to marry him. They walk in the park and he proposes as they are resting side by side on one of the waterside benches. He is too nervous to face her head-on. He need not be; Peggy has long been ready for the question. Given the triumphal tea party and the heavy opulence of his home, not yet aware of Rosemary's hostility and swept away, she tells herself, by Cecil's earnest passion, acceptance is the obvious choice.

Next they need some form of marriage ceremony. Cecil has persuaded Peggy there should be no family presence, neither hers nor his, and Peggy, for her own reasons, is glad to agree. But when he posts the banns in a dingy registry office unknown to both of them and secures a couple of slight acquaintances to stand witness, she begins to waver. Until now she has coasted toward becoming part of a couple, assuming it will all come good. Now it's as if a light has come on which lets her see the one thing she has known all along: this is not the man she should marry. But things have gone too far and she has her pride, and anyway, how bad can it be?

Their first night booked into the honeymoon suite of an exclusive country inn begins well enough – discreet service, nice food, expensive wine – and Peggy's optimism revives. It carries over while they change out of their dinner clothes and into very new and carefully chosen nightwear – she, in the dazzling bathroom, slides into a smooth rayon sheath; he, facing the bedroom wall, buttons himself into opulent striped pyjamas. But when she emerges, ready, striking a glamorous pose in the bathroom doorway and flashing that smile, those incredible eyes, Cecil feels an aggression like nothing he has known before: this is his *wife*; *his* wife. He tears at their clothes and mounts her like a goat, without hesitation or tenderness.

Peggy knew there might be pain and blood (she has read of these things), but nothing prepares her for Cecil's transformation – his awful face, his dreadful intrusions; the shocking *sliminess* of the man. She fights free of him, heaving him off her and on to the floor. She locks herself in the now hateful bathroom, too angry to cry, swallowing great gulps of air so as not to faint. *Breathe*, she tells herself. *I must breathe.* She runs the bath deep enough to drown in and buries herself in the water.

Cecil is mortified. He hates that he has hurt her, and hates her for repulsing him. He sits on the ruin of the bed, staring at the bathroom door until all energy and every sort of passion has left him. Then he knocks quietly: "Diana, my love, are you alright?"

The door stays closed, but she responds with Peggy-like cheeriness: "Yes, yes. I'm fine. Go to bed, Cecil, dear."

Obedient, he slides into dreamless sleep.

Immediately after this (it is a month after that decisive mother-son breakfast), Cecil and Peggy come back to the house as man and wife. Rosemary shows no surprise, and even less pleasure. She is sitting at one end of the buttoned leather divan in the drawing room, making as though to study an art auction catalogue. She makes no move to rise when they come in or when Cecil approaches; she turns her head away as he bends to kiss her cheek and turns it back only to examine his outer condition. Peggy she ignores entirely.

Richard, in a rictus of good manners, rises from his chair by the window, nods slightly towards his new daughter-in-law and mutters something like "Ah, there you are." He moves as if to shake his son's hand, but thinks better of it. And Peggy is left standing in the doorway, beached on the edge of the family island.

This small scene is the template for domestic relations in the weeks and months that follow. Rosemary takes a tight-lipped, stiff-backed, chronically disapproving lead, and the household follows it. The housemaid is especially wary: Peggy is close to her in age and class, but as the young master's wife she is beyond the pale of girlish exchange. The cook and the gardener are older – old, even – and less vulnerable to disapproval, but the cook confines herself to kitchen duties, and while the gardener, bless him, does venture an avuncular interest he will chat only when the madam is out, and only about trees and flowers.

So Peggy is fed, housed, and largely ignored. Invisibility is a new experience for her. She makes every effort to fight it – to be present, charming, useful, seen and heard – but nothing much changes as the weeks pass. Her trademark vitality begins to erode. Cecil sometimes thinks he should try harder to change his mother's attitude. He loves Peggy – as they say – in his way, but the feeling sours when he fails to make her happy; when *she* fails to be happy. Rosemary encourages the idea that the failure is Peggy's, that Peggy is not worthy of him. Cecil stops calling his wife Diana.

No surprise that sex between them is never better than a disappointment. Peggy resigns herself to unpleasant intrusions, not expecting delight, thinking about other things; Cecil knows he should do better, yet firmly believes it is Peggy's fault that he doesn't. When she falls pregnant, both of them are relieved that her 'condition' gives them a reason to quit the charade of their lovemaking. Cecil takes to gratifying his own want, needing Peggy only to lie naked on the bed, untouched, but paying attention to his performance. This remains their formula even after the child is born.

A child. The news of it raises different phantoms of possibility across the family. Richard imagines a male heir and his lineage assured; he doesn't admit the chance of a girl. Cecil welcomes Peggy's pregnancy as evidence of his manly competence and boasts of it among his colleagues; he now fancies himself a successfully married man. Rosemary has little interest in Cecil's fantasy; she is immediately and wholly absorbed in scenarios of his child's future. She doesn't doubt that she will be the one to raise it. This child's life will be her task and her triumph. Peggy and Cecil are not fit parents: one too strong-headed, the other weak-willed…

Any reference to Peggy in these imaginings is dismissive. If interest or concern is voiced – Richard is solicitous in a medical sort of way ("Any morning sickness? Proper diet? You're a good strong girl.") – it centres round the foetus, not its mother.

And what of Peggy? Her first reaction to 'the news' is one of surprise: how could those inept and messy fumblings have led to conception? Beyond that, she isn't sure. She sends a postcard to her parents – *I want you to know, but please don't answer* – but the connection with them is too pale to anchor her. A baby might be a lovely thing to have, to hold and cuddle, but she feels this one has been imposed on her. It was never her idea – maybe Cecil's, maybe Rosemary's, maybe even Richard's; it is a *Siggs* baby, not hers. From the beginning they treat her gingerly, as they would an incubator. Without discussion they seem to have agreed to deny the emotional power of this pregnancy. Peggy catches the point like a virus: incubators have no maternal feeling; she is not *involved* in this motherhood business. Even late in the pregnancy she doesn't identify with the child; doesn't wonder about its gender or play with names it might be given like you're supposed to. And once it is born (male, vigorous, beautiful) she knows – Rosemary makes it plain – that the incubator is of no more use.

Peggy remains seven years in this limbo.

Rosemary stays true to her convictions and manages the care and training of her grandson from the start. An impeccable professional nanny is recruited a fortnight before the birth, allowing her time to prepare the layette and other essentials to infant wellbeing, and to establish her dominion over nursery territory.

The baby is christened with all ceremony, given the names of his father's grandfathers, patrilineal first – Derek George. Peggy ventures no objection, but might have done if asked. Albert's father was called Jack and she liked him as well as his name. Derek is brought to her breast and taken away from it by the nanny on schedules worked out with Rosemary. When he gets old enough he is trusted to Peggy for an occasional playtime in the garden or a bedtime story, but he is not hers to bathe or feed – "You need to rest, dear" – and outings to throw bread to the ducks in the park are normally accompanied – escorted, supervised – by the nanny.

But not everything is awful. Peggy has access to the sheer wonder of contact with a growing child. Even if she ranks behind the grandmother and the nanny in the line of responsibility, Derek chooses her company over theirs if given the chance. She is softer and livelier, and funny. Interactions among the grown-ups have settled to routine: Cecil is cordial and mercifully undemanding; Richard, besotted by his grandson and charmed by the pretty thing who produced him, smiles at her as they sit to breakfast and dinner; and if they meet coming or going in the dim hallway he will sometimes pause to chat for moments on end. And Rosemary? Since Peggy has lost or subdued those initial excesses of vitality Rosemary begins to hope that she may after all be improvable, capable even of learning a few essential skills. When Peggy shows enthusiasm and a sort of talent for needlework Rosemary's goodwill extends to giving her guided access to the sewing room.

Peggy sees this version of home life as a backdrop for things that might happen beyond it, much as she remembers life at home before Cecil came on the scene. She is no surer now what those other things will turn out to be, but the pieces begin to float into focus. For the first time ever she has a room to herself; a bed, a chair, a table, a window with garden views. No one enters without knocking. For a time Cecil made regular visits, but now less and less: perhaps he's getting it somewhere else; more likely he's drained by junior partnership tasks in the Siggs practice. No matter: in this, her own space, Peggy draws variations on what she has seen in Rosemary's pattern books and art catalogues and begins to be happy. The time is not awful and it is not nothing.

One summer afternoon she is walking through the city, too absorbed in thought to notice the route she takes or the effect she has on young men idling in the sun. She is not yet twenty-five; the mere thought of happiness brings back enough Siggs-faded glow to catch the eye. Without intention Peggy fetches up at the dressmaker's shop where she once worked; the same woman runs it, recognises her, beckons her in, makes tea... And another piece falls into place. A couple of afternoons each week – one when Rosemary plays bridge, the other when she visits her sister – Peggy works in the shop to turn scraps of material left from the better dresses into arty

cushions and tea cosies and matchbox covers, which the
dressmaker's customers are increasingly glad to buy.

It can't go on like this; Peggy knows it, and once the story
is known, so does Rosemary. Her outrage is terrible:
she has been deceived; despite her kindness the girl has
contrived to take advantage of her. She... She orders
Peggy to give up this disgraceful nonsense – or else...
Her mind fails her. Peggy's rushes forward: or else what?
Or else she must give up the family.

The idea flares in her mind like a forest fire. She
will divorce Cecil, or let him divorce her. She will move
away and build a business and be independent and make
a life for herself and her child...

This is the impasse: about the child, no negotiation
is possible. Divorce fine, moving away splendid, but
Rosemary will not compromise the boy's future: he
belongs with her and her husband and son in the family
home. The men say nothing; both women read their
silence as support for Rosemary's diktat – she vindicated,
Peggy despairing.

Peggy knows no reasonable way to decide between
her child and her life. If she stays, there is tomorrow and
all the tomorrows with nothing of her own – not the
artwork and certainly not the son. Not even his presence:
when he turns eight he will go to boarding school in the
Siggs tradition and she will see him like a stranger two or
three times a year. If she leaves she will always own the
smell of his neck and the way he laughs.

So Peggy leaves her son with the people who own

him and sets out for independence. In the early months she suffers dreams and disapproval. Her family offer no comfort. She discarded them once and they have written her out of their lives; by now there are other reasons not to let her back in. Lottie is gone with the drink, Albert is swamped by his wife's condition and money worries and backache, and Violet and Winnie, married to good, sexist working men, can't let themselves be sympathetic. It is sinful to abandon a child, unpardonable when he is our nephew. No use trying to explain why he wasn't really hers – theirs.

So she stops talking about it, eventually hardly thinking of him, and plunges on alone. As the spectre fades, so life begins to happen; the four-square personality sidelined for survival in the Cecil era revives. Nourished by energy and talent and a certain manipulative charm, her little business prospers. Alongside it, suitors come and go. She learns what sex can be if you choose a proper man, eventually marrying the most diligent of the suitors, one David Jenkins, again a doctor embedded in the finer things but wittier and more assured; clever in bed. They settle into a satisfactory and largely faithful union. She has two children in quick succession, becomes expert in home interiors and antique furniture and learns to play competent tennis.

Decades pass. The small boy that Peggy left becomes a man. The story picks up when he comes out of conscription in the army and decides to find the mother who left him all those years ago. It is contact with 'other' kinds of people that has inspired him. The conscripts are of every background. In the boring moments between manoeuvres they exchange anecdotes about childhood and home life which open Derek's eyes to the narrowness of his own.

By now his father is beyond contact and the grandparents have died, but he is still ruled by them. Looking for escape, he changes his name and emigrates to America; the mother-loss conundrum travels with him. After one divorce and two changes of career a psychotherapist helps him see what he should have known: if his mother didn't fit in that life, if his mean-minded family had only negative things to say about her, then – logically – she isn't like them; knowing her will let him see what else he is.

His letter is addressed to Mrs Peggy Jenkins and posted from California. It arrives with the morning post and waits at the breakfast table with the newspaper and a couple of bills. The name disturbs her: she stopped being Peggy and became Margaret many years ago. She opens the letter and the Jenkins teenagers, sulking over cornflakes, are startled by her shriek. They have never heard the Peggy backstory, or of this phantom half-brother, and aren't much interested.

But Peggy feels the phantom spring at her like an animal. She is at first winded by it, then confused, fearful, intrigued, joyful... by the end of the day, mostly joyful. This is the missing piece: rejecting her child has worked in her like the rejection of her self – every success tinged with the prospect of failure, every gain with the fear of loss. Now that her son chooses to know her she sees finally what she has always known – that she didn't choose his absence.

There follows a period of intense exchange. Peggy writes to him and reads his replies in a kind of swoon. Frankness invades her. Derek must know the miserable detail of that marriage, understand why she abandoned him; know what it cost her. Derek answers in kind. He wants his mother to know his life, to accept his failures, heal his wounds. They are as eager as lovers, each so self-absorbed that neither hears what the other is trying to say.

It is easy to be in love at a distance, and to be nervous about meeting. It needs fate to make it happen: Derek's job lands him in Europe on a minor errand and the Jenkins' home is only a detour off his course.

On the day of the visit Peggy is coiffed and dressed with special care; her husband sees her shining with the old vitality. At first sight Derek is smitten: this lovely woman is his mother. Peggy's reaction is immediately less ecstatic: she sees a young-middle-aged man too much like his father; awkward and without social grace. Within the hour her need begins to evaporate, and by the time they sit to the celebratory lunch she is no more than a gracious hostess facing an awkward guest. Derek tries to be amusing and the family tries to like him but neither effort succeeds: he finds them stilted and unfriendly; they find him boring. From Peggy they have learnt not to tolerate a bore.

After lunch they cover the tension by taking

pictures of one another; Derek wants souvenirs of his moment with Peggy. The mythical mother-son union is represented in a photograph which shows them together, handsome and happy in a sunny garden. This time Peggy is not troubled by the mismatch of image and reality. This pose is her choice. So is the coming separation; this time she is choosing to reject her son. This time the pieces fit.

Protected

Protected. A protected species. Not, they said, endangered. But why protected if not in danger? Protected against what?

Ours is an ancient stone cube of a house standing by itself half a mile off the road. This is the best of the Dordogne: rolling hills pocked with trees of every green; three farms visible, sometimes audible. The farmer calls his cows home; they answer; dogs bark.

The house is restored, but not quite. Its terra cotta tile roof is edged with a line of modern gutter, but the stone wall of the building doesn't reach high enough to meet it. There's a variable gap of wall that should have been filled in but isn't, wasn't, because it makes a ledge which the owls discovered before we got around to it. Barn owls. In French nature books they're called *chouette effraie* – the 'frightened' owl. 'Frightening' would make more sense: at night their legs, breasts, underwings and faces shine ghostly white, their eyes huge, agate black, and their special and only noise is a snoring hiss; the sound of a bad-tempered crone trapped in the attic – nothing like birdsong; aeons away from the *twhit-towoo* of storybook owls. Locals call them simply *dames blanches*.

There aren't the barns they need anymore, barns with nestworthy spaces that haven't been fixed. So our gap is prime residence and the same tenants claim it every spring. They stay silent and asleep on the long ledge all day, waking to hunt in wide circles across the fields as soon as it's dark enough to see. They lay their eggs up there, regurgitate feather-balls of rodent remnants on to the terrace, eject streaks of excreta down the front wall, teach their young to swallow and hiss and sway and stare, raise them right... until, late August, they nudge them off the ledge into the depths of the grown-up world. Last summer we witnessed the launch, eating supper by moonlight and a candle outside – loud hissing; then two thuds. The first youngster landed in the field next door and gathered himself into a running take-off; the second plummeted straight to the terrace, stood stunned a moment, then hop-limped on to the wall and took off like a glider into the trees. Most years you know the launch has happened only because the night's rhythm changes when the young start to hunt. Their cycle marks out the summer for us.

This year was different. Late May, too much rain and the grass uncut when we arrived, but the usual noises under the gutter. Second morning in, however, W's eye is caught by a dazzling white globe, round as a large grapefruit, posed between the cut stones at the corner of the house. He assumed it was a mushroom – what else grows so big overnight? – and gave it a passing prod with his cane. It stirred, ever so slightly, and we saw it as a breathing ball of fluff, comatose in the light, fallen from the nest.

In all the years we had never met a baby *chouette*. What to do with it? First thought was protection – from rain, sun, hawks, a passing dog. I readied the green waste paper basket with a bed of dry grass and put on the gardening gloves. Grown-up *chouettes* have the beaks and claws of nightmare; our baby was rolled in on himself so no sharp bits showed, but we could assume he had them. Indeed they were there, but lifted in my two canvas hands, everything – eyes, beak, claws – was closed; inert. Put down in the basket the ball adjusted to the space, a child snuggling back to sleep, but it barely moved.

The Yellow Pages gave a number for animal rescue. You could hear dogs barking when they answered.

"No, we don't do birds. Anyway, for *chouettes* you need the Office of Protected Species. I'll find the number. Did you try putting it back in the nest? Too high? Do you perhaps know someone with a ladder?"

G, of course! Our friend and neighbour, a man of the countryside and a builder with ladders for roofs! He wasn't home; we left the same urgent message in three places. The Protected Species woman was calm and full of facts: sometimes the baby has toppled out. If food is scarce the young lean out too far as their mother arrives with a beak full of mouse. No, she won't come to feed it on the ground. She may have pushed it out: maybe it's defective, runty; maybe she just feels she has too many.

"We mothers can understand *that*." The Protection lady laughed primly. "If so she'll shove it out again – but

once is worth a try. Feed it first if you can. Raw meat –
chicken or beef," she said; "never lamb or pork. And…
I wish you the best with this. It is good that you called
us…"

We were chopping up bits of chicken gizzard when
G arrived, fairly running from the gate with the ladder
over his shoulder. He unfolded its three segments with
a shocking industrial clatter and extended them three
floors up above the owls' landing place. Finding nothing
there, he cursed, came rapidly down, clanked the ladder
round the corner to the front face of the house and ran
again up the rungs, urgent as an ambulance driver. At the
top this time, he went calm.

"Here," he said. "Ahhh. So beautiful. There are two.
Staring and swaying. They are small but very lively. No,
no parents around. But lots of stinking evidence."

Back on the ground, he turns at last to the fallen one
in the waste paper basket. He's a big man with a back
the width of an omnibus, but he bends over it like a new
mother. The bird lies inert on one of his bare hands –
playing unconscious again? Dead, maybe? We pry open
its beak, but it makes no kind of response to the bit of
gizzard directed by toothpick towards the back of its
throat.

G says, "I think it's no good, but we should put it
back in case. We should try…"

Still holding it in one hand, the other moving up
the rungs ahead of him, slowly now, he went again
up the ladder and placed the ball beside its swaying
siblings. Immediately it unfurled into a bird and scuttled

energetically to the furthest end of the nest. *Maybe it's fine after all?* G came down, fast again, and collapsed his ladder.

"If it stays up there now we will know we have saved it," he said. "Otherwise…" He left, already with other priorities on his mind.

But it didn't stay up there. Next morning, there was a biggish snowball glowing halfway up the slope at the back of the garden. Same inertness in the hand, but back in the waste paper basket, this time it stared hugely at us and raised its claws to its chest as though preparing to attack. We backed off, putting it in the shade with the orange apron spread over its plastic nest so that it might respond, owl-like, to daylight and go back to sleep.

Meantime, M in London searched the internet for barn owl trivia. Her searches confirmed that there's no point putting the baby back a second time, that they are very difficult to feed and unlikely to survive in human hands – although it has been known, so it's worth a try… But there's new information on the rescue receptacle front: owls are happier looking outwards into the landscape, rather than upwards out of a hole. And they should be given a tea towel to sit on so that they can grip something: hay is not helpful.

So we converted a six-bottle wine carton into more bijou *chouette* accommodation, with a towelling cloth at the bottom, air holes punched into the top, and a small rectangular window big enough to look out of on one side. Our resident showed no interest in anything until dusk, when there were scuffling sounds behind the cardboard. *Surely it was hungry?* By now we had defrosted a supply of prime minced beef, softer than giblets, maybe easier to swallow. But again the creature went inert in our hands, not limp – inanimate more like. Forcing open its beak made space for a glob of meat in its mouth, but there was no reflex; the bird stayed motionless, its beak held ajar by food. But back in its box it seemed to swallow. After twenty minutes it began again to agitate, so we took it out and repeated the grotesque feeding ritual. During the evening, glob by glob, it got through as much as a teaspoonful of food. When it began to hiss – only when alone in its lair, of course – we convinced ourselves there was strength returning, a chance of survival even. We put the box outside, wedged between two trays, and went to bed optimistic, suppressing the guilt of violence inflicted in the cause of nurture.

In the night I was haunted by my mother insisting, towards the end of her life, that she was not to be forced to live. In the early morning I wanted somehow to apologise, to explain myself, to the lovely, helpless thing that had fallen into our hands. But there was no point. Somehow the creature had forced its way out through the small hole in the side of the box. It lay elongated right next to the box as though it had fallen dead from the window.

English Spaghetti
(Basutoland, 1963)

Over the weeks it has dawned on her that old Zack's effort
to make an English garden is not as much about making
those unlikely flowers grow as it is about making her
happy. He smiles and nods if he catches her eye. There's
none of that somehow threatening servant-to-madam,
black-to-white, forelock-tugging flattery she can't get
used to. When it comes to the garden, she and Zack are
on the same side. Squinting against the glare, she can see
him scoop half-cupfuls of water from the bucket with
his tin ladle. He is careful not to waste it, trickling one
measure on to each precious, wilting English thing. His
back is dense with conviction: the plants will thrive with
a little water and a lot of loving concentration.

They both know this isn't true, that a thing reared
for soft rain and gentle summers cannot thrive among
these jubilant red-orange xerophytes. No more than her
pale-white children can adapt their skin to the African
sun. No more than her husband Brian can adapt to the
stones thrown at his car in the name of Independence.

The failure of the flowers says all this. Old Zack knows it too, but never mind the outcome, he persists in his effort with the misplaced seedlings to make up for all the disappointments. It is his way of willing Ann and Brian and the children to feel at home in his place. They are *his* white family. Just as each ex-pat family talks of "*our* Africans", they belong to him and to Mary, his wife, who works in the house. Each family cares for the other in its way. Their children combine like siblings. Zack and Mary's eldest goes to the two-room Mission School across the valley and their younger ones play at doing chores behind their small, round house at the end of the garden. Ann's brood go to Government Primary near Brian's office. Home in the same garden at the end of each school day, the two sets of children reconnect. Cricket is the current favourite game.

Brian had organised a mail order surprise to fix her homesickness. *For an English Country Garden* it said on the packet. *Amenable to all garden conditions*. When the seeds first arrived she remembered the happy song. Now it drones in her head:

> *How many kinds of sweet flowers grow*
> *In an English country gar–ar–den?*
> *Daffodils, hartzies and flox*
> *Meadow sweet and lady smocks…*

She tries to suppress it. Alright. This is no English garden, but it is a good garden for round here. Tidy, at least, thanks to Zack. At home *she* was the gardener.

Here, this morning, every morning, she stays out of the heat and watches him at work. He labours so diligently to make it look like the picture on the seed packets. He fills buckets of water from the tank outside the kitchen, humps them across the spongy kikuyu grass, all the way over to what he calls "England's beds" under the thorn trees which form the western fence. Every morning the same pattern, and at the same speed. It's hot, and he isn't young, and every sensible African knows not to hurry.

Her reverie is broken by Mary, standing quietly in front of her. "The children soon come, madam," she says. "I have made the table ready." They thank each other – Ann for the preparations, and Mary for leave to make food and eat with her family in their neat outside kitchen area. It's the same every school day; a cherished routine. Mother-love is reason enough for a woman to want pieces of time alone with her own children. Ann imagines that Mary must cherish moments when *she* is the one in charge; for herself Ann has learnt that practical chores done without help make threads of continuity with her so-distant English life – which, come to think of it, is close to the same thing.

So Ann moves to do what needs to be done. Lunch. Today, she will make something special – not the usual picnicky, processed cheese or peanut butter sandwiches she puts out for their midday meal. She will find a treat to make her children smile. Her throat contracts with wanting them to feel at home in this alien place.

Most things in the food storage cupboard are tediously ordinary: condensed milk, custard powder, bully beef, Mazawattee tea, sardines, corn syrup… Rummaging at the back, she finds the perfect thing! Two large tins of Heinz spaghetti in tomato sauce. She had quite forgotten about them.

A car door slams and Ann gets to the front window as the children wave goodbye to Brian's driver and turn eagerly towards the house. She watches them – her own English flowers – coming across the dry garden. Ben and Harriet are walking quickly, side by side – most likely discussing some scandalous happening at school, deciding what and how much to tell her about it. At nine and eleven they are old enough to have secrets. Peter, always apart from the others, weaves a slow path in big loops from left to right, studying the ground. Soon he'll be six and will go to the big school in a matching uniform. Maybe then he won't feel so left out.

The flame flares under the spaghetti as they clatter into the kitchen. The two big ones start to talk at once: "Mummy, guess what… and you know… and then he… It was so–o–o funny…" They go on talking in the scullery, washing their hands in the basin of water which Mary has made ready, with soap in a saucer and a clean towel on the stool. They are laughing together now, drying themselves at opposite ends of the towel.

Peter, meanwhile, stands at her side. She can feel the slight leaning of his body against her hip. She hunkers down to hold him, smiles into his face, pats his bottom in the direction of the basin and announces that lunch is a special surprise.

They sit in their regular places in the too-formal

dining room, Ben on one side of the heavy table, Harriet and Peter facing him. Ann's place is at the kitchen end, next to Peter. When he's home Brian sits opposite her, at the head of the table. That's usually only breakfast and supper, but every day Mary sets his lunch place with the others anyway, on the rare chance that he'll get home from Government Office in time. She has drawn the shutters against the midday brightness, hooking them at a shallow angle to let in a stripe of glare down each centre. Light reflects off the polished furniture and the children's pale hair. In Ann's imagining, the children light the room.

She lifts the lid off the casserole and they stretch their necks, trying to see through the steam, making a show of sniffing the lovely smell, mmmm-ing. Ann basks in the moment of dishing up: this is something she knows how to do, has always done. She serves them in order of age – first Ben, then Harriet, then Peter – and they wait for her signal so that everybody begins at once.

Today, after the start-up noise of spoons and forks, there is silence for a couple of mouthfuls. Then crowings of delight – from Harriet: "It's *lovely* Mummy!", and from Ben: "Can we please have this again tomorrow?"

But from Peter…?

She looks at him and the others stop, mid-mouthful, to see what she sees: Peter, rigid against the chair back, is staring in horror at his plate.

"Peter?"

He says nothing.

"What's the matter?"

He is transfixed by the long white strands in their blood-red juice. Ann leans across and takes his near hand, shaking it a little to break the spell. His stark face turns briefly towards her, but his eyes go back to the plate.

"What is it?" he whispers.

"It's spaghetti," she says brightly. "It's Italian."

Now Peter begins to cry. Ann feels a surge of irritation, then a ludicrous sense of failure. "For goodness' sake!" she says. "What?"

Between sobs, Peter gulps, "I don't like Italian."

Ann's chair rasps on the floor as she gets up to go to him. Standing behind Peter's chair, she takes the spoon and fork out of his suspended hands and chops the spaghetti into stubby pieces, banging the plate, criss-crossing it, first one way, then the other; the way you cut a proper lawn. In no time the dish is domesticated. She lets out a long breath, sets down the utensils, straightens up and steps back.

"There you are," she says briskly. "Now it's English."

Peter relaxes. With a small smile he takes up his spoon and begins to eat. Ann suddenly knows how she will deal with the alien garden. She goes back to her place and they all get on with lunch.

Scandal

The road ran parallel to the train track, straight as a rail. I could see her as soon as she turned into it, a pretty woman, name of Violet, with hair red-glint when the sun shone, pushing the pram lightly up Station Hill, pausing only to bend to the child or show her off to someone she knew. She came into view most days just before the *Express* went through – just when I needed a lift: starting before six at the fruit market, by teatime I'd been up for hours and was sagging. She'd stop to chat and maybe buy a piece of fruit, choosing carefully, never bargaining. It felt good to discount prices without saying anything, without being asked. She wasn't poor, mind you – neatly dressed, the toddler tidy and rosy in the buggy. It was just that her presence made me generous.

That afternoon she appeared as usual, smiling at the child and the day as she progressed up the hill. As she levelled with the station a woman came out from it. Violet waved hello, all friendly. But her face changed as the woman stepped stoutly into the pram's path, put one hand on its handle, holding it still, and gestured wildly with the other, pointing at the child inside.

I missed the next bit, deflected on to the weighing of potatoes and Bramleys by a serious customer. When I turned again the buggy was a few feet away and coming fast. Violet's head was bowed over it. She looked up when she reached me and her face was twisted with a terrible anguish.

"Look after her," she said. The words were a choke. Then before I could speak she ran from me and disappeared into the station.

I heard the train scream. Afterwards they told me Violet was on the track in time to meet it.

The Four Square Gospel Church is a short mile away from the small terraced house where Violet lived with her husband Russell – a plumber by trade – two shock-headed ginger sons, Russell Junior and David, and their much younger sister Eunice, who had brown curls. The children were clean and polite, Russell serious and sober. Violet herself was "a good little woman". Her only fault, Russell liked to say, was that she's a bit of a seeker, always looking for a better way to be. One time, before Eunice was born, she thought Spiritualism might be it, even missed church to go to a séance or two, but that blew over and she turned back to the Four Square Gospel. Russell didn't attend with her. Sunday was his only day off work and anyway, religion is not for men. Violet went alone or in the company of her friend, Mrs Bray, a widow nearing middle age who claimed to be "like family". One whole summer she lodged in the house with them; at that time she told me, coyly and with a dainty laugh, that she was especially attached to Russell himself.

In those days the sign on the mission hall proclaimed three services on Sunday and private prayer sessions by appointment with Pastor W. C. Lockyer. The services were well attended and fervent. The pastor's flock was especially enthusiastic about baptism by immersion, the laying on of his hands to heal the sick, and the possibility that he or his congregants might speak in tongues. During these rites the hall grew intimate with sweat and noisy with hallelujahs. No one questioned the rightness of the tithe they owed for the work of the Lord, even though few could afford to pay it. And if anyone suspected the pastor of salting the church's money away they didn't say so out loud.

Violet was among those who sought extra solace in private prayer with Pastor Lockyer. Her visits to his study passed unremarked: Violet was a good woman whose devotion only confirmed her Christian piety.

Of course Violet's death devastated the family; Mrs Bray moved in to help them through it and stayed. Speculations about the suicide in the congregation were slow to build. Mrs Bray helped them along, observing aloud that little Eunice was quite unlike her brothers. See how her eye colour and head shape match Pastor Lockyer's? And the same small ears! Once she'd pointed out the resemblance, others could let themselves see it.

At first the swell of feeling was all about poor Violet, peppered perhaps with gentle tut-tutting over those private prayer sessions. Hard to pinpoint when the mood changed into that swell of hostility against the pastor. The congregation turned on him like piranhas. Adulterous paternity was only the first of their accusations. Scandal seeped out over his finances, his neglect of the old, his touching up of girls during Sunday school – all misdemeanours that people had always known but no one had let themselves see until then.

The effect on the Four Square Gospel Mission was catastrophic. Within a short time it was closed down, the congregation disbanded and Pastor Lockyer disappeared. I don't know where he went. About that time I retired and moved to the coast. I saw a piece about it in the local newspaper.

Now it is twenty years since Violet ran up Station Hill to my stall. There is no more speculation, no sign of that turmoil. The hall has been demolished to make way for shops and offices. I think of Eunice. Does she ask whom she resembles? Does she care about the truth? Does anyone know it?

From this distance it doesn't matter. The old pains are buried and I see no reason to dig them up. I shan't come by here again.

Mothering

In all the years I can't remember a child not feeling better after I hugged it, or a small baby not calming in my arms. Newborns especially. Frantic birthlings passed to me by their frantic mothers just fold into me, into my breast, with something like a sigh. It's a gift that has blessed me: nurturing feeds warmth and comfort back to you. Until now, anyway. Until them.

It was late yesterday evening, during that rain, when the doorbell rang. I had just put my supper on the table and damned whoever it was for getting in the way of it. I could see him through the spyhole. He wore a baseball cap backwards, like they do these days, and the rain ran down his face. Peaky-looking, and the rest of him thin in a faded windbreaker and too-big jeans. Wet. He looked familiar, but I wasn't sure from where. He gave his name as soon as I opened the door. Anton Lewis, he said. But that didn't help; only when he said he was in my lecture class I understood that I'd have seen him as one of more than a hundred students.

Mostly, if I'm truthful, these young people are anonymous. But I do have concerns for them, for their confusions and impossible plans. Seems they sense it, or maybe they tell each other. I don't turn anyone away; there'll be a steady trickle of the troubled young in my office, on the phone, sometimes – like Anton – here at home. What I feel for them is a pale version of my feelings for my own children. Mine are older than these, and distant, but still I want to make things better for them. The young man at the door was – is – nothing like my son, but clearly he needed mothering. Seeing him dripping on the doorstep I felt that protective surge and waved him in.

He was carrying two packages. One was a plastic supermarket bag which he dropped inside the door; the other a bundle held tight in the crook of his arm. He followed me to the kitchen, leaving a trail of water behind him down the hall. When I handed him a towel he dabbed briefly at his face, still holding the bundle, and was impatient to give the towel back. I did think he should take off his cap and rub his head as well, but I didn't say so. Neither of us was saying much at all.

Anton set his bundle on the kitchen table; in the light I saw it as a rolled up blanket. He unwrapped the rough grey outer layer to show a fluffy pink package inside. He gestured at it.

"I need you to keep her," he said. "Just till tomorrow. There's milk and stuff she needs in that bag." A pause, then an afterthought, doubtful: "We might call her Jenny – but not yet…" Strange he didn't look at his child as he said it.

Of course I picked up the small cocoon and moved

the pink blanket to see the baby's face. Tiny, pointy features, a bit blotchy, clearly very new, quite inert, only squinting against the light. Anton watched my face with his red-rimmed eyes. I looked back at him.

"What of the baby's mother?" I asked.

He seemed to sag with the question, and mumbled something I couldn't hear.

"Is her mother alright?" I wondered about hospital, maybe a damaging delivery – death, even.

He drew a long breath. "She's gone away."

"Run away?" Now I had visions of domestic violence.

"No, no." This time he was firm. "She went because she doesn't like the baby…"

Oh God.

"And… and she says it's my fault!" He lowered himself into the chair furthest from me and the baby. He covered his face with his hands; I could hear the snivelling. I felt irritation more than anything and turned away to make a pot of tea. The baby held herself stiff on my arm.

By the time I got back to the table Anton had sniffed his way to a kind of composure. The tea drunk – he wouldn't eat anything – he jerked out his story. The baby arrived three weeks ago, everything normal, and he and Sara – "She's called Sara" – took her on the bus to their small apartment. Sara couldn't or wouldn't breastfeed so it fell to Anton to check out bottles and formulas. Quite soon he was doing all the feeding and changing and Sara "just turned away". The worst was in the night. Every night the baby shrilled and screamed and wouldn't be comforted, and Sara screamed, "Shut up, shut up!" and locked herself in the bathroom…

So now she's gone away and Anton must find her and bring her home. He thinks he knows where to look, that it won't take long, that he – they – will come for the baby tomorrow.

So I said, "Alright, I'll keep her for you." I told him not to worry; that soon the doctors will fix Sara and the baby will learn to sleep in the night. Perhaps I believed it myself.

Once he was gone I could focus on the baby. I made a nest for her, blocking the edge of the kitchen armchair with its cushion. I know babies don't roll at that age but I wouldn't take the chance. I placed her in the nest, tucked in warm and comfortable, lying on her back. Her eyes were open like before, still squinty and looking at nothing. Still she didn't move. I leant over and made cooing noises.

"Hello, my sweet one. Don't be afraid. Everything's fine. Your mummy and daddy will come for you and love you and care for you and everyone will be happy…" I used the tone of voice that babies warm to. Most babies. This one's eyes moved toward the sound but her face didn't change. Is she wet? Is she hungry?

At that point I still expected it all to come good. Given the years of mothering and my talent for it, how could it not? I got busy unpacking Anton's plastic bag: milk formula in a box, a bottle and teat, four disposable diapers, a Babygro suit with a rabbit motif. The kitchen sink is the right size for a baby bath. When it was half full and the water mixed I tested its temperature with my elbow. All the things practised mothers do without thinking. I undressed the baby gently; her clothes were wet and stale and her scrawny nethers were flushed with the beginnings of nappy rash. I stroked her back, made murmuring and shushing sounds... Even in the water with her head cradled on my hand the little body stayed rigid. Quite suddenly that blank, flat stare of hers began to feel like hostility.

I dried and dressed her and set her back in the nest. She whimpered a bit then – the first sound I'd heard her make – so I knew she was hungry. It takes time to prepare a bottle, even when you know the steps like I do: boil the kettle, sterilise the bottle, measure formula into it, add hot water, shake the bottle, hold it under the cold tap to cool, test the temperature with a few drops on the inside of your wrist... By the time it was ready the baby's whimper had risen to a steady whine.

Normally a cuddle and a bottle work like retuning a radio – out of complaint and into contentment. Not this time. True, the baby grabbed at the teat, gumming it, sucking half the bottle down without a pause. But then she lay back in my lap, rigid again, stretching her legs. The strange eyes fixed on mine for a second before she let fly a terrible howling, loud and shrill, the sound of ancients keening for misery and loss, sharp to set the soul on edge. Wind, no doubt. I raised the little body over my left shoulder and rubbed and patted her back with my right hand as a mother should. I was expecting the sound of a belch and then I would say, "'That's better. Well done. Clever girl", and I would smile into her face and we would both be relieved.

But it wasn't like that. If there was a belch the howling masked it; there was no telltale relaxing of the little body and no letup of noise. When after what seemed like minutes it did stop, the silence lasted only long enough to let the baby fill her tiny lungs and launch again.

I tried everything: all the wind-breaking positions, all the ways of setting her down, picking her up, jiggling a dance, singing a song. More than once I checked her nappy. I tried ignoring her. I tried to eat. I sat at the kitchen table with my back turned to her armchair and took a spoon of the pasta congealed on the supper dish, but my throat closed against it. I even tried leaving her in the nest and hiding in the hall. Nothing made a difference.

Of course I couldn't give up. Better at least to move her about; a changing scene might in time distract her and steady movement could calm both of us. So I took to walking around the house, up and down the stairs, stopping in front of every picture, every light, every mirror, anything that might hold her attention. Nothing distracted this baby. The terrible, shrill keening set my teeth on edge and slashed a migraine across my eyes. It expanded to fill the house and left no room for escape. She did pause, twice, to suck down a feed of formula, and both times I breathed deep and hopeful as she drank, but the quiet didn't last; every small respite topped up her strength and drained more of mine.

The night passed in a building nightmare. As daylight came we fetched up in the bathroom and I stood with her in that bright light in front of the mirror. In the glare my face was lined and yellowish, and not as I knew it. I heard myself burbling feebly, stupidly – "Hush now. Hush. There we are together. Look at us… There now. There…"

All at once, just then, looking in the mirror, I saw why all this mothering effort had been futile. I knew it when her eyes caught mine in our reflection and she paused and held the look to show me the hostility in her, the baby venom; as though she wanted me to see the glint of triumph on her vicious little face. With all that keening and howling, there was nothing the matter with her. At least, nothing a mother could fix.

Now that I knew the sound for what it was I knew I had to defend myself. There was no help for it, nowhere without it. When I blocked my ears and couldn't hear it, still I knew it was there and it made me afraid. It filled my head till I could think nothing else. Till I was no longer myself…

Till the baby went quiet.

I gave her mothering and got nothing back. Now I am empty of it and all I can feel is tired. Maybe I should sleep till they come for her. I will try to be strong. To comfort them. To help them know what she was and what has happened. To explain… Maybe they'll be glad.

Red Carpet

Grace still hears her mother saying it: "Death is the second most important thing to happen to any of us." So when she saw the notice of Mme Lascaut's funeral she prepared herself to attend the village church at the advertised time. The young priest nods to her as she enters; she is a reliable mourner and he is grateful for that. Sitting always halfway down at the side, her face shining ebony in the stony light. No one pays her attention.

When Grace and Aiden first took up residence, people were cautious. It must be curiosity that brought them closer. What else could you be in the face of such a couple? That marvellously old Englishman in his baggy shorts, socks under his sandals, the hat tied under his chin with a scarf to keep the sun off in case of skin cancer. They have even grown used to his ebullient African wife, younger, much louder, much more outgoing. By now they are just another pair of locals at the Friday market – Aiden nodding and smiling from his great height, carrying Grace's basket of shopping, padding along behind her. And she greeting everyone in her bad French accent, bargaining hard without the vocabulary to name the vegetables she wants to buy. But never offensive, she hopes. Just curious, you could say, in her turn.

Now Grace wonders at the sparse turnout for Mme Lascaut. There in the front row, that must be the husband and daughter. A few rows behind, two grey women sit close together, bent toward each other, talking discreetly; a third sits alone midway down the aisle. There is a group of four young people with rucksacks in the back row – cyclists probably, using the cool church as respite from the hot afternoon. They don't stay to accompany Mme Lascaut to the cemetery across the road.

Grace walks at the end of the small procession, some paces behind the three women. Ahead of them the little family follows the coffin on its gurney. They are near enough to touch it, but both hold their arms tight to their sides. Two of the women lean hard on walking sticks; the third steadies the weakest with a hand under her elbow. Grace resists offering help: Aiden has said that Europeans don't like to be touched. She concentrates instead on the litany of the priest leading the coffin, and the rhythm of the censer swung by his diligent altar boy at the front. Two cars pause to let the procession cross the road, and a bearded man in a hurry holds his baseball cap to his chest and lowers his head as it passes. Otherwise the afternoon is undisturbed.

Next day Grace has prepared one dish of strong meat and one of sweet dough to strengthen the family. They are not close to her in any family way, but in the days after a funeral, proper people will support near-ish neighbours and fellow villagers as though they were. Death, where Grace comes from, belongs to everybody. After lunch Aiden goes for his siesta and she sets out to do her part.

This is her first visit to the Lascaut farm. She knows which house it is – the one so low in the valley that only the roof is seen from the road. She parks her car at the top of the overgrown track. A mailbox planted up on a stick for the postman's convenience says *Lascaut* in faded ink on a yellowing card. Grace sees it as the boundary of the house. To cross it by car without warning or invitation would be an assault on privacy. So she makes a slow pace down the track in the hot sun, shifting the heavy dishes in the straw basket from arm to arm.

The wooden door is wide open but she stops and calls – "*Koti, koti*" – the way proper people knock when there are no doors. There's no response, but now it is polite to proceed. Coming in from the dazzle it's a moment before she sees Monsieur Lascaut and his solid daughter – Sylvie, isn't it? – sitting at the table in the dim kitchen. They are shockingly alone. Not even Madame Lascaut's body is there to comfort them. The funeral has left them blank.

Sylvie rises with effort as Grace comes in, standing with her palms flat on the table, leaning into it. She doesn't offer her hand, doesn't approach. Her face is blotched with grief and she keeps her eyes averted. The old man is past noticing, past politeness anyway. He stares steadily at his fists on the table, at one thumb mechanically stroking the nail of the other.

Grace lifts the covered dishes from the basket and sets them on the table. The pretty pattern of cherries and birds on the oilcloth makes her suddenly sad. She feels it as she limps through the condolence in her foreigner's French.

Sylvie says, "*Merci*"; her father says nothing. In the awkwardness Grace hears herself babbling, but no one responds, not really; it's just that every time she pauses, Sylvie mutters another thank-you. She seems not to notice when Grace's recital of sympathy turns into excuses for leaving so soon. Sylvie sits down heavily as Grace turns to the door. The old man still hasn't moved.

Out in the brightness, gloom covers her like failure. This is not how death should be marked. Unmarked. She feels responsible; in her homeland every person is responsible at such a time. If there is no one else then she, Grace, must find a way to honour Mme Lascaut, to bring comfort to this silent little family.

She worries at these things as she trudges back up the drive. Suddenly, mid-trudge, she thinks of inscriptions on the war memorial in the village square. Of course! Mme Lascaut must have a memorial! She stops abruptly to focus the image. Not a monument. No. Better a living thing. She remembers a tree which grew in the centre of the family compound at home. They say her great-grandfather planted it, that each generation following must nurture it, that even to sit under it in the peace of the evening honours those who have passed. She sees herself as a child, blessed by them, playing in its shade.

Grace moves off slowly as her plan begins to simmer

and it has time to set before she gets to the car. Yes. She, Grace, will plant a tree in Mme Lascaut's honour. She will make a plaque and mark it with Mme Lascaut's name. She will invite the three old ladies from the church to witness the ceremony. She will help them all to mourn properly. Yes.

The surviving Lascauts are unenthusiastic. Monsieur is almost truculent: "It's not *my* plan," he says. "It's not what *we* do. I see no reason to plant another tree. The land is already too much work…"

Grace waits. She has persuaded the young priest to come with her and hopes he will now find the right words. He says nothing. Nothing he learned in the seminary prepared him for this kind of standoff.

After a heavy minute, Sylvie, suddenly animated, leans forward and speaks up. "But I think," she says, "I think Maman would like it if she knew."

Her brief energy fades into dreary sniffling. But this mention of the newly-dead brings the priest back on cue and he crosses himself, murmuring the litany. The others follow, two beats behind him – father and daughter mechanically, Grace with some fervour. She sees a break in the impasse and steps solidly through it.

"Supposing, Monsieur – if you will permit – we were to plant Madame's tree on the escarpment of *our* garden, where it looks over your farm, where we could tend to it without troubling you?"

The grunt of M. Lascaut is non-committal. The priest tries to engage him by reference to Christian generosity, but truthfully, the old man is not interested.

Sylvie tries too – "Papa? *Pourquoi*? Papa?" Another heavy minute, then once more his apathy releases her. She turns towards Grace, her chair rasping on the wooden floor: she knows the escarpment; she can see the tree in her mind. "Could it be pink?" she asks. "Maybe an *arbre de Judée*?" Her face is bright with the image.

With help from Aiden, Grace Googled it to check the look.

> *Arbre de Judée originated in Southeast Europe and West Asia. This small tree is a delight to see in spring, when it is covered with rose-purple pea flowers. They appear in clusters all over the plant, even on main branches and sometimes the stem. Even when heavily pruned or pollarded the plant will continue to flower throughout the summer. In the autumn the 10cm leaves, which are thin, and round or heart-shaped, turn yellowish-brown. It grows best on hot, dry, rocky soil, reaching a height of 10m...*

The local nursery adds a practical note: *We are unable to deliver bare-rooted trees during the summer months. You may still order bare-rooted trees for delivery in the autumn (from October).*

Perfect. But then a horrifying sideswipe: *L'arbre de Judée is known in English as 'The Judas Tree' since legend has it that Judas Iscariot hanged himself on it.*

The image of pink flowers is suddenly eclipsed by

the shadow of the traitor dangling from a branch. Our Lord betrayed. Who can be honoured by the thought of *that*? And yet… And yet, the tree blooms beautiful. Grace stares out at the dry, silent French landscape and thinks of funerals in Uganda, the sound and the smells – all that singing and wailing and feasting to honour the departed. So different. Here the church was empty, the husband surly, the village absent. She straightens her shoulders. Alright. This is the way they are. If indifference to Mme Lascaut's death has dishonoured her life, so the pink blossom will celebrate it. Anyway, Sylvie wants *this* tree.

Alright.

It is early November, chill and unusually wet. The small tree is leaning against the sliding door of the verandah, balanced on its bare roots, yellow-brown leaves drooping damply against the glass. Aiden says it looks sick. Yesterday he called it a "damn poor show". They sit side by side, watching the rain.

Grace is disconsolate. Weeks ago she chose the planting site and organised the builder's son to dig a proper hole in it, but now, three days before the scheduled ceremony, the site is sodden and the hole has lost definition. Aiden is asking what else he can do. Already he has scheduled the boy to plant the tree, identified a vintage bottle for the after-toast and arranged to collect Mme Lascaut's three mourners in his elderly car on Saturday morning. Sylvie, of course, will make her own way up the hill. The rest are uncertain: M. Lascaut has yet to acknowledge the happening; the young priest is not sure he can get away from his proper Saturday duties in time, but he will try. Does Grace want Aiden to rustle up more people?

She says it's the wet that worries her, not the numbers. Umbrellas may protect hats if it is still raining, but what about shoes? It's a twenty–metre walk through thick mud from the hard standing to the tree site, and those women are unsteady enough on the dry. Back home the rain would drain away as it fell and there would be kinsmen to lay wide leaves along the path. Aiden takes her hand. She knows that for him it's not about the Lascauts or the old ladies. It's about her following him to this alien place and her refusal to give up on making it good.

"Your plan can still work," he says. He has remembered a roll of red Turkey stair carpet waiting in the garage for the attic extension – or a rainy day (he snorts at his joke). "We will use it the way your people use those leaves," he says.

Grace looks at him in a kind of wonder. How good he is! The mixed images become a movie in her mind: a red stripe dividing the sea of mud; the women solemn and dry-footed: a slow procession wending up to the little tree; the priest's blessing, then a libation poured at its root and more on the verandah afterwards. Yes.

And so it went.

War Torn

The war started just as my student visa expired so I couldn't go home when I was supposed to. They said I didn't qualify for refugee support because I'd been in London too long, and that without a visa I had no legal right to work.

"So sorry, Anya," the woman said. "We will review your case next year."

The worst part was the helplessness. Every day the news reported awful things about Bosnia. I feared for my brothers and my parents and their neighbours, but mostly I worried about my sister, Beta. She was born when I was ten and I've always looked after her. All I wanted was to bring her to me in England, to see her safe and happy.

There are jobs you can get without a permit. I started with house cleaning for the Woodfords. Mrs Woodford saw my card in the newsagent's. She was kind; she said I should call her Ruth. The first weeks she tried to teach me to clean but I wasn't good at it. One day we sat down over a cup of tea and she told me I should go for that waitressing job in the local Spaghetti House.

"Tips," she said. "Doesn't matter if the wages are bad, tips will push them up and over what you could ever make swabbing and ironing for us."

The manager said yes immediately. He didn't care about permits. "How can I resist you?" he said. "A classy brunette like you, my dear, with cheekbones and those lovely tilted eyes…" Turned out he was only talk.

As the tips rolled in life did get easier, but I couldn't shut out the horror of news about Bosnia. Every night I dreamt of Beta in danger. Every day the papers and the TV pundits discussed 'ethnic cleansing' and mass rape as if it was binge drinking or foxes on London streets. I felt no one cared enough to *do* anything. But what did *I* do? I kept up a cheerful restaurant face to cover the shame of my helplessness…

Then one day as I dashed among the lunchtime tables, Marisa came in. She looked the same: taller than me, blonder, rounder, familiar as a sister, best friends at school, in and out of each other's kitchens for all those years… Now here! Marisa on a lunch break, now with a job in the supermarket across the road, never been in this restaurant before… The luck of it! We laughed and cried over the din of the eaters, shrill enough to make the greasy manager frown. We vowed to see each other often, often.

Whenever we met we talked about home and London and exile and, quite soon, about how helpless we were to protect our families. I'm Croatian and a Catholic; Marisa is a Muslim Serb. This makes us ethnic enemies. What can friends do about *that*? One evening, over a bottle of schnapps and a pizza in Marisa's bedsit, we made a solemn agreement: as long as the two of us didn't quarrel, *ever*, as long as our friendship held strong throughout the conflict, then our two families wouldn't be harmed in it. Of course we knew the pact was only childish magic; of course the fear didn't go away, but it's always better to do *something*. And who's to say: when now the war has ended without damage to either family, who's to say the magic didn't work?

By the time of the ceasefire I had been 'regularised'. I'd saved up the travel and support money and signed the papers to make Beta's way into London clear and legal. Mrs Woodford found us this flat. It's near her house: two rooms, a tiny bathroom, the kitchen a cupboard in the corridor. It came with two narrow beds, a sofa, a square table with a Formica top and two chairs under it. When Beta arrived Mrs Woodford drove me to collect her at the airport. It was wonderful! Immigration passed easily, no luggage was lost, and all the way to London we sat side by side in the back seat, clutching each other like hikers in high wind.

We settled together comfortably. Beta stepped into the housework niche that I had escaped and found a talent for it that I never had. I carried on darting between the restaurant kitchen and the crowded tables – except now I smiled for contentment as well as tips. On days off sometimes we explored London, but mostly we stayed at home watching Mrs Woodford's old TV with the sound turned down so we could talk and talk and talk. Two topics came up a lot: my beloved little sister was growing fat but making no effort to monitor what she ate. I tried hard to know the reason for it – not nagging, of course, only concerned. The other topic was Frano; Beta only wanted to talk about Frano.

She had met him only weeks before she left Bosnia and I knew about him from our mother's letters. He is a Serb and fifteen years Beta's senior. Neither was a cause for anxiety – at least his family is Christian. Mama said these things as though asking what *I* thought about it. Truthfully, I wasn't sure. Of course I wanted Beta to be happy. But she talked so much and so fiercely about Frano that I began to wonder if she was worried by something about him.

One day over supper, Beta said, "You know how Frano writes me two letters every week? Well, today's letter…" Her face went red. "Look, here, I can show you the words. See? Frano says he wants to be my fiancé. Can you imagine? I'm so happy! I know you think he's much older and we don't know much of each other but you should see how handsome he is, how loving, how strong. He does say we will marry. Maybe when I am older. Anya, look, here, he says he must come to England so we can be together, properly engaged, until I am ready… Darling Anya, I do love him!"

Tears flooded her round cheeks and she sobbed noisily. I held her, patted her back – did all the things that used to comfort her when she was little. Finally, she took two hiccoughing breaths, blew her nose and was calm. I was in turmoil. A man we don't know wants to come to

London and take her away and she will be heartbroken if he doesn't. But I told her I would try my best.

Frano arrived in a flurry of news and suitcases. He had wild russet hair, wide shoulders and a spade-shaped beard. Even Beta said she didn't remember him so *big*. The two of them were to take over the bedroom while I slept on the sofa. The plan was that Frano would get work that needed no language – but he would quickly learn English, settle and move up the migrant ladder. And Beta would be happy.

For three or four days everything was lovely and cheerful. Then Frano fell into a deep lethargy. He refused to leave the flat, even to go shopping, and spent each day hulked in front of the television. Evenings, he hardly spoke; ate, it seemed, without pleasure, and at night (Beta whispered it) he did not behave like a man in love. It broke my heart to see Beta flirting and cajoling to bring him back to her.

Then after a month, she changed tack. "So why did you come? You said you loved me. Look at you now! What kind of man behaves like you?"

Frano remained passive until this last jibe: "What kind of man behaves like you?" Face livid, he lunged off the sofa and raised his arm. As Beta screamed his name he turned from her, staggering into the bedroom. We heard him sobbing on the other side of the door but were too afraid to follow. When he came out he was sweet and sorrowful – he didn't mean it, he would never hurt her, he does love her – but the connection didn't last. That night he thrashed and shouted in his sleep, and next morning he was back on the sofa but instead of staring at nothing he took to chewing the back of his thumb. The nail was soon raw; he seemed transfixed by the bloodiness of it.

I saw Frano's mood spread over Beta like an infection. Now two of them sat like mourners on the sofa. Frano grew agitated if Beta moved out of sight; mostly he was calm with her beside him. I once saw her smile when he took her wrist and held it with his unbloody hand. Each day left me more anxious. At night I would lie sleepless on the lumpy cushions, blaming myself, desperate to *do something*. Round this time I wrote to tell Frano's parents of his state of mind. I didn't spare them the crazy details or play down my desperation. When people at work asked what was the matter, I couldn't tell them, and I kept clear of the Woodfords. Soon I had closed out everyone except Marisa; she had been my friend through everything.

Marisa persuaded me that Frano must be mentally ill, that we must get him to a GP. She said she, Marisa, would organise it and would persuade Frano to go; maybe the fact that they are both Serbs would help. At the flat, she took one of the two kitchen chairs and sat knee to knee with him, talking softly in their mother tongue. He looked up and nodded. She talked some more; seemed to ask a question.

This time he said, "Yes, yes." After the next question

he shook his head, *no*, and turned back to the bleeding thumbnail.

In the end Frano agreed to ask the doctor to fix him, but still he wouldn't tell Marisa the matter. She backed off, put the chair back in place under the small table, gave me a hug and went off to make the appointment. It was during her working hours at the supermarket so the three of us went without her. When Frano's name was called we crowded with him into the doctor's room, me to speak and translate, and Beta so that he wouldn't be afraid.

I tried to summarise. The doctor said, "That thumb looks nasty", and Frano let him dress it. The doctor asked those routine questions: "Bowels? Waterworks? Temperature? Joint pains? Sleep? Ah! Bad sleep? There it is!" The doctor wrote a prescription: one pill with food every evening, come back next week if the patient doesn't feel better.

As I took the prescription from him I asked politely, "Maybe Frano should see a psychiatrist?" The doctor, flustered, cleared his throat, said, yes, normally he would refer such a case to mental health, "but since this poor boy doesn't speak English there would be no point". As we left Beta and I thanked him and Frano tried to shake his hand. The doctor smiled vaguely, said, "Good luck", and called in the next patient.

Back at the flat, Frano said he didn't believe in pills. "That doctor knows nothing of my life. How can I talk to such a man?" This was the first time Frano said he might want to talk at all!

Marisa was encouraged. Someone had told her of a Serbian priest in south London. "He takes Mass in Frano's language, confessions, even... He and Beta could go together."

"Yes," said Frano. "Yes."

On Saturday Frano, Beta and Marisa went by bus to the church with the Serbian priest. I couldn't get time off work. Marisa told me afterwards how it went.

The priest was glad to help a fellow Serb. Frano stayed alone with him for more than an hour. On one of the stone benches outside, Beta told Marisa that her feeling for Frano was gone; "He has become too strange." She said she was more afraid of what he would do if she left him, of how I would feel after so much effort to bring him over...

Marisa assured her that I would be relieved. As for Frano, they must make a plan. "Maybe the priest has learnt something that will point a way?"

Frano emerged from the meeting brighter and friendlier than we had seen him in weeks. He told Beta how kind the priest was, how fatherly, how good to talk to. Marisa discreetly asked the priest if Frano had revealed his problem.

"If he has," the priest was solemn, "even if he *had*, the sanctity of the confessional forbids my telling you what he said." Marisa was contrite; he relented a little. "Perhaps," he said carefully, "perhaps the poor boy would be better back in Bosnia."

Now it seemed the only thing keeping Beta with Frano was the fact of his presence; even the priest had said he should go home. *Will Frano agree to go? How can he travel in that state? Is there a way to fix him long enough to get him away?* At the end of the week we still didn't know what haunted Frano and what we should do.

Frano's father's reply to my letter answered both questions. It was written over several pages in an old man's spidery hand. He started with greetings and regards, and thanks for welcoming his son. He said he would have been delighted to receive Beta as his daughter but can see why it was not to be.

> *Frano was a good boy until bad things happened. Please, after what I have to tell you, please remember that…*
>
> *When the war began the young men from here went together to join the army. They were excited. They thought only about the chance to be a hero. The leaders talked about 'cleansing' the country. They said things would be better without Muslims. No one knew what 'cleansing' could mean. Frano joined with the others. They were full of spunk and bravado.*
>
> *Many weeks he was away. We heard nothing. We could only pray. I do not know what happened to him, or what he did. He never spoke about it. But I do know he was at Kalinovik that terrible time, and I imagine the worst. He came home changed, his eyes sunk deep in his head, screaming and shouting in the night.*
>
> *It was better when your sweet Beta came into his*

life. We were hopeful when he went to England to be with her. We thought the old Frano was coming back. I see now we were wrong. My son is damaged. Perhaps if he comes home and can be with friends who saw what he saw and can share his guilt, maybe then he will recover. He can work on the farm with his brother. With God's help we can take care of him here. I am sorry you have been so profoundly troubled. I hold your family in my heart...

So. We sat over coffee in the back of the restaurant; I read the letter and passed it to Marisa. Marisa was stunned. Frano was involved in the butchery of Muslims; how could she now look into his face? For some moments she focused on the surface of her coffee as if trying to read it.

Then she straightened, breathed deep and took my hand: "We must focus on practicalities. Beta must not be told of Frano's past, at least not now, and Frano cannot know in advance what we have in mind."

Since meeting the priest he had been pacing the flat, lumbering into the furniture, still afraid of London and now openly homesick.

He was delighted by the idea of taking his fiancée on a visit to his parents. He washed his hair and trimmed his beard. Beta was firm in her resolve to leave him, and yes, she was prepared to fly with him to his father and come back by herself.

The problem was, if Beta set foot in Bosnia she'd lose the refugee status that let her stay in England, so that was out of the question. They would wait weeks for visas into Italy or Austria, and anyway, might be refused; Germany was tight but it did allow a forty-eight-hour turnaround for family reasons like this.

We finally agreed that Beta and Frano would fly into Munich and Frano's father would drive from Sarajevo to meet them. It is far, but his other son would come with him and they could stay overnight with his wife's cousin on the way. Frano would then drive back to Bosnia with his father and his brother as Beta got on the plane for London.

But where was the money for it? We three women scrimping for a month might manage enough, but a month was too long; Frano's agitation was building. So I went again to Mrs Woodford, told her the story – well, part of the story – and asked to borrow the ticket money.

"Of course," she said.

We booked two tickets to Munich: one single, one return.

Departure was calm. In the air Frano held tight to Beta's hand and dozed the whole way. As they landed he began a kind of whimpering which, by the time he reached his father's hug, had risen to a shout. After the greeting and hugging and laughing and kissing the four of them sat on a bench in the airport lounge to catch a breath. While Frano quizzed his father and his brother for news of home, Beta excused herself to go to the ladies' room. The last she saw of Frano he looked happy.

When I met her at Heathrow she was tired but radiant. I didn't ask about Frano. Back in the flat, Beta began to cry. I couldn't comfort her. She cried for a week.

The Shirt Collar

It is a fine autumn evening, dark but not late. Our son Keith is watching TV with his best friend Duncan. Their two heads are bent close, one Africa-dark, the other Danish blond. I break off making supper to answer a heavy ring at the door. Theo, who runs the Greek restaurant, is revealed, red in the face, breathing hard. He holds a brown-and-white check shirt collar aloft in his fist, waving it like a flag.

"Look at this! Look at this!"

The policeman stands behind him and to one side. His face is smooth. He takes his helmet off when I appear, bobbing a little bow – must be new to London – and begins a hesitant: "Sorry to disturb you, ma'am, but this gentleman…"

Theo wades in over him: "Your son did it." He is triumphant. "This time I have proof."

I back up the hallway to make distance between my face and the thrusting piece of cloth. Theo follows me, advancing over the doormat as though invited in, nodding thank you without pausing his anger. The policeman extends his arm as though to stop Theo's progress into the house, but pulls it back mid-stretch to replace his helmet.

As though on cue, Darcus erupts into the hallway. The men have long known each other, but are never friends. "Who asked you into my house?" says Darcus to Theo, in the Trinidad way. Theo moves back to the doormat, still talking, explaining, accusing...

Darcus notices the policeman and tempers his voice: "Is there a problem, Constable?"

The young man has remembered the rules of no entry and retreated all the way outside. In truth he doesn't know what the fuss is about, only that there is 'an ethnic conflict' afoot and he risks being caught in its crossfire. His account of events is muted by anxiety and Theo's override.

Eventually Darcus gets the picture. Theo has grabbed a black boy who was defacing the chalkboard menu outside his restaurant, tearing the collar – "this very collar!" – off the boy's shirt as he fled. This was not the first offense; Theo is tormented too often: "Fish and chips £1,000 instead of £10; rhubarb and cus-TURD... The officer has seen it with his own eyes, yes?"

The policeman nods warily. Theo says he always knew the guilty child was Darcus' son. Now he has proof – here, in his hand!

Darcus knows his son, knows him capable of many things, so he doesn't argue the case. Instead he turns the accusation on Theo: "You've molested my child," he shouts. "Torn his clothes! Assault is a criminal offence. Maybe not where you come from, but in this country

I can bring charges. You dare to break into my house talking foolishness about a menu…!"

At this point the two men are talking at once, both hot with indignation, each embroidering his own version of blame. For them the shirt collar is no longer in contention. Suddenly it is for me: now that it hangs loose in Theo's hand I realise that it's not part of any shirt that Keith has worn; that that brown-and-white check has never belonged in our family.

My first thought is to say so, to put a stop to this crazy duet. My second is more cautious. Maybe it's Duncan's collar? Maybe Theo, distraught in the half–dark, had Keith in his sights but it was Duncan under his hand? I mutter about pots on the stove and leave the scene; there is no pause in their haranguing.

The boys look up, startled, as the door to the TV room bursts in on them. Their programme is playing so loud they have heard nothing of the fracas in the hall. I turn it down so they will register what I'm saying.

"Duncan" – I look him in the eye – "show me your shirt." Aha! He is alarmed! His blue eyes widen and he looks afraid!

Although when Keith says, "Mu-um?" in that two–syllable *for-goodness'-sake* way I realise his poor friend may simply think I've lost my mind.

Duncan is encased in a bright green sweater with a turtleneck collar; no other top is visible. He gets up from the couch, edging away from me just in case, and peels off the sweater. Under it he is wearing a stripy yellow

T-shirt which plainly never had, is not supposed to have, a collar. He clowns to cover the fact that he has no idea what I'm about, standing at mock-military attention, his ten-year-old chest pushed forward, looking sideways at Keith to make sure he is laughing.

I am embarrassed. "Right," I say. "Thanks. That's alright then." I leave the room, trying to look purposeful.

In the hallway Darcus and Theo continue to jostle for alpha status but their wrangling is quieter – now more like a courtroom argument than a street brawl. They must be tiring; they must want the situation resolved. So does the policeman. He is still standing in the doorway with a notebook in one hand and a stub of pencil in the other, ready to write definitive things down if they should occur.

The smell of spaghetti sauce simmering in the kitchen gives me heart. "Listen," I say – my voice is stronger than usual. "Listen to me, Darcus." The three of them turn. "It's a mistake." Now I'm telling all of them: "That's not Keith's collar... It's nothing to do with us. Somebody else's boy must've done it. Someone else's child got grabbed."

All three are now staring at me, motionless and silent while they take it in. The puff sighs out of the two fighters; even the policeman is deflated. After a moment, in a kind of unison, they flex their shoulders to slough off sheepishness, squaring them as though ready to move on to whatever important thing each had been about to do when he was sidetracked.

Theo turns toward the door. The collar is flaccid in his hand. He shoves it into his pocket, steps over the threshold without looking back, says, "Good evening" to no one in particular and proceeds – resolute, straight–backed – down the path.

The policeman looks at him, then back at us. He makes another little bow – "Sorry to trouble you" – and turns to follow Theo into the street.

"OK, man." Darcus mutters it, shutting the door behind them.

He follows me into the kitchen; he will not speak until his resentment is recharged – I know the signs. He flings himself into a chair, snapping open the evening paper – for effect, I think, not for reading.

After a minute he shuts it again, folds it neat on the table, stands up, says, "Bastard!" – not too loud, but building; and again, "Bastard!" He bangs his fist on the table. Now he's in full flood: "In bloody Theo's eyes every naughty child is black and every black child is ours. Bloody racist!" He pushes his chair in hard and stands very still; I see from behind his hands on the back of it and his shoulders tense with thinking.

"Darcus…" I try.

He lets go of the chair and turns, blank-faced. Then his shoulders relax and his face cracks a slow smile. "Did you hear him?" he says. "Cus-TURD!" He snorts. "Cus-TURD! That's a good one!" And he starts to laugh.

Darcus is proud of our son.

Square Dance

High on his stony plinth at the south end, Lord Russell keeps an eye on them – tourists, children, students, office workers and street people, moving round and past each other. He sees the best of squares! A public garden in the city centre with 300 year old trees, a ring of handsome Georgian buildings and a fountain which spouts in random heights and rhythms from its cement floor. There's a café with outside tables. There are pigeons to feed and squirrels tame enough to climb up your trouser leg and pose for a selfie…

Tourists know of the Square from their guide books. They dawdle through it as they cross from the underground towards the museum. On sunny days not a few will give up on the cultural bit of today's plan and settle on a bench to watch the children and the dog walkers and the Frisbee players, entranced by what they take to be Englishness…

For children the fountain is the draw. The braver of them try to block the water jets; littler ones paddle round the shallow edges, running out to their parents when the water threatens to wet them and shrieking with delight when it does. Some go into it fully clothed, some have come ready with their small bathing suits, others run about in their knickers. One, yesterday, cavorted in a sagging nappy. No one is naked; even the visiting Swedes accept that in the Square you must cover the sex of your young.

Students lie about in twos and threes, sleeping off the stress of studying or celebrating the end of exams. The office workers take their lunch break here: some buy food to eat at the cafe tables but most bring plastic boxes from their separate kitchens, setting them out on someone's jacket spread on the grass. When it's cool enough, there will be joggers. The Square is more encouraging than any gym. And free.

Then there are the street people… They may notice the water and the green bits, but for them the architecture of buildings round the great space is what counts.

In the beginning we felt privileged living here, even if below street level on the 'lower ground floor'. This means that out of our front windows we see the bottom of passing legs, not the verdant tops of trees, and that our entrance is down a lethal run of concrete steps, quite separate from the main door to the building on the 'raised ground' above.

In our building this door is flat to the front wall. This is true of each alternate building in the stately terrace. The doors of those in between are set back behind a portico which forms a sheltered space with one open side. The design has that classic symmetry admired by architects and it makes a fine backdrop for visitors wanting photo proof that they really have been in historic London. They pose on the steps. They find the grand entrances bespoke to their needs. So do the street people – but for them the need is a secure place to sleep. For them this setting scores twice: once for the porticos, once for safety. Posh neighborhoods are safer than rough ones.

Most nights there'll be a clutch of sleepers somewhere along the row. Mostly they cause no bother. Only our building is residential: the rest are offices which close by six o'clock and leave the handy doorways clear for settlers. In twos or threes, just after dark, they salvage the large cardboard boxes put out by the offices for the recycling truck. If they're lucky the cardboard is dry and there's enough of it both to screen a dwelling space against the street and to line its tiled floor against the chill.

Mostly they have moved on before even the keenest secretary appears; the soft-spoken Colin from Camden Street Safe does an early morning round to get them up and out. Every day he reminds anyone conscious enough to listen that they could have a bed in the local hostel-for-the-homeless – and/but, of course, he says, it is their choice… Sometimes they curse him but aggression is unusual. Mostly they simply shoulder their valuables and straggle off to spend the day in the crowded concourse at King's Cross.

Being on different schedules the sleepers and the office workers rarely meet face to face. But most mornings one or other smart secretary will face the spoor of sleepers' rubbish in her office portico: slabs of cardboard, an empty booze bottle, old newspapers, forgotten clothes, the suspicion of urine… They complain to each other, tutting over lunch in the grand garden, or standing on their separate front steps for a smoke. Any sign of over-nighting spreads agitation up the terrace and draws the women together; the detritus of street people unifies them like new gossip.

In our 'lower ground' hole we stay apart, telling ourselves that the homeless cannot be blamed for every affront to hygiene, that the bits of rubbish and acid smells in our front patio could be the gift of drunk or drugged or thoughtless people lurching past along the pavement. No matter who causes it, we tell ourselves, cleaning up jetsam is a location tax we pay for living in the lovely Square.

But some taxes are excessive. One morning I opened the front door to make out a pile of human turd, dim under the roof created by the main steps of the building. The shitter – presumably the very shitter – had partially covered it with newspaper, but not enough to contain the stink. I retreated inside, closed the door, leant back against it to bar the 'thing' coming in, panicked. What to do? How to get rid of it?

Once calm enough to breathe I called Camden Council Environmental Services. No: it wasn't their responsibility. Sorry: they only deal with matters affecting public property; private patios are off their limits. I tried

Camden Street Safe but the kindly volunteer said nobody volunteered for 'that sort of thing'. Sorry. In the yellow pages then I found a firm offering 'Garden clearance and rubbish removal' but when I told them the nature of my rubbish they backed away. Absolutely not, the woman said. Not at any price.

In the end there was nothing for it but the dustpan and a black bag and the power hose and I cleaned it up myself.

It is late Sunday morning some days later. I am climbing the steps into sunshine and a walk under the ancient trees – pretending I don't notice the settlers in next door's entrance, not wanting to see into their privacy, to see things I might not like – when a cheerful voice calls *Lovely day, don'cha think?* It's a sane voice. Friendly. So at the top of our steps, where the iron railing ends, I turn to greet back.

The caller is one of three men set up in next door's portico. He's at the front, sitting in the sun on the step outside its roof. I can see another behind him, crouched on the entrance floor, nodding moodily at nothing. The third is stretched out along the door, asleep or unconscious; there is a sheet of cardboard over his legs. The front man's face is sun-dark, black in the creases. I cant see hair: he's wearing a blue-ish woolly hat.

Yes, I say. *Lovely morning.*

You live down there? – gesturing towards our hole.

Yes we do.

Hope we don't bother you none, he says, all neighbourly.

Well no, I say, being neighborly back. Then, remembering, *But I wish you wouldn't throw rubbish over the side.*

'Ow dyu mean?

Well, there's the cigarette butts and wrappers and stuff… And – I feel shy about this – *there's even been pee through the rails.*

That's never us, he says. *We use a bottle. See here…* He raises a plastic Evian flask half full of something yellow. I am not deflected; I've started so I'll finish. *And last week, even, someone did their business by our door.*

They never! he says, appalled. *That's never us. We use the public one there by the park gate. Paying and all!*

I don't want to think about it.

I ask him how long he's been living on the street.

A couple of years on and off, he says. *Since the army. All of us is veterans. There's nothing for veterans. No jobs, no houses, no respect. Bloody government – Cameron, is it? – does everything for the bloody immigrants. Country's overrun. After we fought for it…*

I don't like where this is going.

Yes, but…

He drives on. *They don't do nothing for us. There's nothing for us but the street. All weathers. Tonight, prob'ly, it'll be cold again.*

I'm sorry, I try. *But there are hostels. At least you'd be indoors. Colin says – you know Colin? – he says they're clean and dry and you get a breakfast.*

He scoffs. *Hostels is full of bloody thieves! Steal the boots off your feet they will. And more.*

There's a pause, then a tailing off.

But sometimes… he says.

I prompt him. *Some nights you might sleep in a hostel?*

Yeah, he says. *Like last week, in that rain, we was over King's Cross.*

And how was it?

'S not the bleeding Ritz, he says. *More like the army. Cold water washing. Weak tea. Worst is they get you up at six, drive you out before seven. Worse 'n cub scouts even. Here's better for that. Sunday morning in the Square no one bothers. We come here of a Saturday night for a bit of a lie-in on the Sunday…*

I have no comment.

You 'ave a good day then, he says, dismissing me.

He shuts his eyes and turns his face to the sun.

Acknowledgements

Most of these stories were inspired by the real lives of people I have known or known of. Names are changed and experiences tweaked to protect identity or to make a better story, but inevitably some will recognise themselves in the characters I write about. Whether or not they do, I have learnt that my imagination can only build on the willingness of others to talk about themselves. I cannot begin to list them, but the debt must be acknowledged.

I have enjoyed the support of our small writing group. We began together under the tutorship of Jacob Ross and continue his tradition of positive critique. Most importantly I recognise my own debt to Jacob as mentor, editor and family friend throughout the process of creating this collection. Blessings upon him!

S.W.
February 2016